Booting up the computer on his desk, Mark had more on his mind than he cared to have

There was a pile of client portfolios on his desk screaming for his attention. Half his day had already been shot to hell haggling with his younger brother, and thoughts of that woman kept creeping into his mind. That woman. Mark's body quivered at the thought of Michelle, the cool chill racing the length of his spine having become too familiar since the two had met.

Mark was finding it difficult to rationalize what was happening to him. Never before had any woman consumed his waking moments the way Michelle Coleman kept invading his mind. Especially not a woman he'd not even had an opportunity to take to dinner yet. For crying out loud, he thought to himself, shifting in his seat, the two had only met for five short minutes, the woman barely giving him a second look. He couldn't begin to believe how love struck he was suddenly acting.

Books by Deborah Fletcher Mello

Kimani Romance

In the Light of Love
Always Means Forever
To Love a Stallion
Tame a Wild Stallion

Kimani Arabesque

Forever and a Day
The Right Side of Love
A Love for All Time
Take Me to Heart

DEBORAH FLETCHER MELLO

is the author of eight romance novels. Her first novel, *Take Me to Heart*, earned her a 2004 Romance Slam Jam nomination for Best New Author. In 2005 she received Book of the Year and Favorite Heroine nominations for her novel *The Right Side of Love*. For Deborah, writing is akin to breathing, and she firmly believes that if she could not write she would cease to exist.

A true renaissance woman, Deborah's many career paths have included working as a retail buyer and size model for a national women's clothing chain; a finance manager for a well-known beverage organization; a sales manager for a candy company; a telecommunications administrator and corporate trainer for a hotel-owning company; an art gallery director for a world-renowned artist; and an administrative consultant for multiple organizations throughout the United States. Deborah is also a licensed real-estate broker and general building contractor.

Born and raised in Fairfield County, Connecticut, Deborah now calls North Carolina home.

TAME A WILD
STALLION

DEBORAH FLETCHER MELLO

KIMANI PRESS™

ISBN-13: 978-0-373-86069-2
ISBN-10:   0-373-86069-2

TAME A WILD STALLION

Copyright © 2008 by Deborah Fletcher Mello

www.kimanipress.com

Printed in U.S.A.

Dear Reader,

I so love what I do! I have been so blessed and I understand that it has been a generous and loving God who has lifted me up and enabled me to do this.

Thank you for taking this amazing journey with me. I know beyond any doubt that if it were not for you this experience would have been short-lived. Your words of encouragement and support continue to keep me writing, and motivate me to write well.

I have been living and breathing the Stallion men for months now and with each one, I am more in love with the idea of love! I so hope that you enjoy getting to know each one and that you fall in love with my Texas boys just like I have.

Until the next time, take care and God bless.

With much love,

Deborah Fletcher Mello

www.deborahmello.blogspot.com

For "Johnny"

Without your strength and support I would not have
been able to get through this. Thank you for your love.
Please know that you have my heart, now and always.

Chapter 1

"There is absolutely nothing wrong with this car," Michelle Coleman intoned, attitude edging her voice as she eyed the man before her. "You keep trying to find something wrong and for the umpteenth time, there's nothing wrong with your car."

Her well-dressed client rolled his eyes, pursing his lips as if his face hurt, the muscles contorting in response. "Mitch, I drive this car every day. I should know when it doesn't feel right," the man responded, calling her by the nickname she'd gone by since she'd been a child.

"Look, Doc, I do the maintenance on this car regularly. At least once a week I've got my head stuck under the hood because you're sure something's wrong and every time I tell you there is absolutely nothing wrong with your damn car."

Dr. Marcus Shepherd bristled, exasperation fueling his words. "Just check it for me, Mitch. Please," he implored.

Michelle swiped her hands on a dirty rag hanging from

the rear pocket of her coveralls. She shook her head, strands of jet-black hair falling from the tight bun she'd twisted at the nape of her neck. Annoyance painted lines across her very pretty face. The three old men watching in amusement from the other side of the room couldn't miss the beauty that peeked from behind the grease and grime she wore like bad makeup.

She heaved a deep sigh before finally speaking. "Uncle Simon, bill Dr. Shepherd for two hours of my time while I check his engine, please," Michelle said, turning her attention to the elderly man who stood patiently behind the desk waiting to see how the exchange was going to play out.

Behind her, Dr. Shepherd nodded eagerly. "Thanks, Mitch, I really appreciate this," the man said softly. "Do you really think it's going to take two hours?"

Michelle shook her head from side to side. "No. I doubt that it'll take me all of two minutes to find absolutely nothing wrong with your car, but since you want to waste my time you might as well pay me for it," she said, moving in the direction of the garage bays.

Dr. Shepherd watched her, his gaze falling on the sway of her full hips as she glided toward the exit. Color suddenly rose to his cheeks as he twisted his fingers together nervously. "Maybe when you're done, Mitch, you and I can go get something to eat or maybe we can catch a movie and then do some dinner?"

Michelle paused and did an about-face. She studied the man who stood eagerly in wait of an answer and then she laughed, her head shaking from side to side. "Uncle Simon, bill the doctor for three hours. It's going to take me at least an hour to get over that stupid question." Her head still waved like a loose ball bearing against her neck, as she turned to face the man, her hands clutching her ample hips. "Doc, I know you've fallen down and bumped your big head now. Is that why you keep bringing this car in here, hoping I'll go out with you?"

The doctor shrugged, his shoulders pushing up toward the ceiling. "A man can hope, can't he?"

Michelle rolled her eyes and moved back through the large doors that led from the office into the work area. She was still waving her head from side to side at the man's audacity, chuckling loudly as she disappeared from sight.

Dr. Shepherd heaved a deep sigh, turning his attention back to the other men, who stood staring at him from the corner. Simon Coleman grinned as he extended his hand, the other mechanic pressing a ten-dollar bill into his palm. Every few weeks Michelle's uncle made the same bet about one of the clients making a play for Michelle and getting shut down fast and hard. His bets had paid off handsomely, ten-dollar bills lining his pockets like gold. If there was any one thing the old man was certain of, it was that his niece could shut a man down faster and harder than any other woman he'd ever known.

Mark Stallion ran his hand across the handlebars of his brand-new Gold Wing, the touring motorcycle a combination of power, luxury and extreme sporting capability. His brother John stood with him, both admiring the classic lines of the Honda vehicle. John had to admit that the dark-blue metallic vehicle with its gleaming chrome accessories was truly a specimen of perfection, if you liked that sort of thing. Mark called it his private jet on two wheels, one of the many expensive big-boy toys he'd acquired over the past few years.

"You're looking good, boy!" John exclaimed, admiring Mark's black leather jacket and pants.

"I'm feeling good," Mark answered, tightening the strap on his helmet. "As soon as I get the bike tuned up I'm out of here.

I'm looking forward to being on the road for a while." He shifted the bike's weight off its kickstand and onto its wheels.

John nodded, understanding his sibling's need to be away. The two had been manning the reins of Stallion Enterprises since forever, the large corporation boasting success with its shipping company, many real estate investments and assorted entertainment ventures. All of the Stallion men, brothers Matthew, Mark, Luke and John were committed heart and soul to the family business, rarely taking time out for some much needed rest and relaxation.

Where John's conservative disposition rarely allowed him any time to play, he greatly admired his brother's fortitude and free spirit. Mark hardly ever succumbed to tradition or directives. Of the Stallion siblings, Mark was the brother with a penchant for fast cars and even faster women, rarely slowing down, as if he were afraid he might miss something in his young life. With over two million miles of paved road across the United States, Mark was intent on satisfying his wanderlust every which way he could and his annual jaunt to the Carolina coast for the black bike festival was only one of those ways.

"Just be careful, and stay in touch," John said, his arms crossing over his chest.

Mark nodded. "How can I forget? You stay on my back about that."

"Just you remember that, too," John said, smiling from ear to ear.

Mark shook his head, a wide grin filling his face. "Look at you! You're gushing!" The man shuddered, pretending to shake his body vehemently. "You're grinning like you're still on your honeymoon, John. Don't get too close to me. That mindset might be contagious."

"You could stand to catch some of this. This is good for the soul."

Mark rolled his eyes, swinging his leg over to straddle his bike. "I don't want any part of that mess. There are too many beautiful women out here in need of attention. I've still got my work cut out for me and I do plan to work hard this weekend."

John chuckled. "I'm sure some woman will slow you down soon enough. I use to say the same thing, remember? Then I met Marah. When that bug bites, it bites hard."

"Sounds like something I need to get an inoculation for," Mark said, laughing. He checked his equipment one last time and then started the engine.

John took a step back out of his way. "Stay in touch. Let us know where we can find you," he said, brotherly concern wafting into his tone. "And keep yourself safe. You're one of my best friends."

"You already have two of them," Mark said, referring to their two brothers.

John smiled. "Three's a charm."

Mark smiled back. "Always has been in my book as well." He gave his brother a quick wink as he adjusted his helmet one last time. "I love you, bro!"

"I love you, too. Have some fun!" John chimed.

As Mark gunned the bike's engine and headed out the driveway of the family estate, John waved his hand after him. Mark waved back. Without a second notion, Mark headed east, a warm May breeze pushing against his back.

The old man had called her twice now, seemingly oblivious to the fact that Michelle was purposely ignoring him.

"Mitch! What are you doing?" Simon questioned for the umpteenth time that day.

The young woman rolled her eyes, still refusing to respond. Michelle couldn't help but think that her entire life resembled the undercarriage of the sports car she was staring up at. The mechanics of the vehicle were pristine, everything maneuvering so smoothly that she almost questioned why she was lying on her back beneath the aluminum frame and Fiberglas body examining the nuts and bolts of it. The owner whining that he was so sure something had to be wrong was the only reason she was now wasting her time.

Most things in Michelle's life were going as smoothly, but it hadn't always been that way. Years had passed since Michelle's life had been a profusion of everything going wrong that could. So much so that she now found herself spending far too much time worrying about what might go awry if she weren't careful, wasting energy that she could have been using elsewhere. Clearly though, her most pressing problem at the moment was her uncle's annoying drone. The man's voice intruded on her thoughts as he kicked lightly at her steel-toed work boots.

"Hey, girl! You all right under there?"

"I'm busy, Uncle Simon. What's the matter?"

"The doctor wants to know if you found anything yet."

Michelle rolled herself from beneath the car, her eyes pressed into thin slits as she stared up toward the patriarch. "Uncle Simon, do me a favor and tell the good doctor I said if he doesn't stop being a royal pain in my…"

Her uncle raised an index finger in her direction, shaking it vigorously as he stalled the harsh words about to spill past her lips. "Watch your mouth, young lady."

Michelle sighed with exasperation, pausing a quick moment to contain her attitude. "Tell Dr. Shepherd that I will be right in," she said finally.

"And there's a man here to see you about his motorcycle. Him and the doctor seem to know each other. He said his brother recommended you."

"Who's his brother?"

The older man shrugged. "That was the one thing he didn't say."

She nodded. "Fine. But he's my last customer today. I want to work on my own ride today if I get the chance," she said, eyeing the classic 1969 Shelby GT500 that sat in the corner of the shop, the floor around it littered with parts and pieces.

Simon tossed her a toothy grin. "Do me a favor, girl. Make that fool ask you out again. I've got another ten bucks riding on it," he said, winking in Michelle's direction.

The young woman scowled. "One day, old man, you're going to lose."

"Not the way you be treatin' these young fellows around here I won't," Simon responded. "A man don't stand a chance with you."

"I just haven't found the right man yet, Uncle," she said, grinning as she rolled herself back beneath the car. "Just not yet," she finished, her voice echoing from beneath the vehicle.

Simon grinned. "Well, then you better hurry up on in here. This boy with the bike actually looks like he can walk and chew gum at the same time. You might get you a real prize if you play your cards right."

Michelle laughed heartily, the wealth of it ringing into the office behind her uncle. "If that's a recommendation, Uncle Simon, I'll pass," she said, both of them chuckling warmly.

Marcus Shepherd was extolling the virtues of Coleman and Son's star mechanic as Simon made his way back into the room.

"I swear there is no one better," the man was saying. Mark Stallion eyed him with reservation.

Mark looked down to the watch on his wrist. "Well, my brother Luke highly recommended him," he said. "Figured now was as good a time as any to see what the man can do."

The doctor grinned. "You've never met Mitch, have you?"

"No. Why?"

The men holding up space in the room all laughed, but before the physician could respond, Simon closed the heavy metal door harshly behind him.

"Mitch be right here," he said, breathing heavily, as if he'd just run a mile-long race. "Doc, you ready to write that check now?"

"We figure out what's wrong with my car?" the man questioned, an eyebrow raising hopefully.

"Like I've told you time and time again, nothing," a deep alto voice responded from the entranceway to the work area. "Not one blessed thing."

Like the others, Mark turned in the direction of the doorway and the beguiling tone that drew their attention.

The female before him cut a quick eye in his direction, catching his gaze and holding it ever so briefly before moving to stand behind the office counter. Mark's gaze followed her, taking in the silhouette that defined her femininity beneath the clothing that did nothing to flatter her very female figure. His eyes widened curiously, his interest piqued as she scolded the doctor, one of his brother John's many fraternity brothers.

"Don't bring that car back in here, Doc. And I mean it. I swear if I see you or that vehicle again in the next three months, I'm pulling the engine and you won't be riding in it ever again. You got me?"

Marcus chuckled. "Yes, ma'am!"

Michelle handed the man an invoice, holding her hand out patiently as he wrote her a check for her services. When their transaction was complete, the good doctor waved goodbyes, and she turned her attention to the man who'd been eyeing her curiously, looking him up and down.

The brother was one good-looking specimen of manhood, Michelle thought, admiring Mark's rugged good looks. The leather attire added to his bad-boy appeal, the ensemble complementing his mahogany complexion, full lips and shoulder-length dreadlocks. But good-looking men in Dallas were a dime a dozen, she mused, barely allowing herself to pause to admire the line of his chiseled features and haunting eyes. "How can I help you?" Michelle asked, her gaze meeting his evenly.

"You're Mitch?" he asked, surprise in his tone.

Michelle dropped a hand to her hip, shifting her weight. "You have a problem with that?"

Mark shrugged, a sly smile pulling at the line of his full lips. "No. Not at all. I just wasn't expecting a girl."

"You didn't get a *girl*," Michelle snapped, annoyance creeping into her voice. "I'm a grown woman and don't you forget it. So what can we do for you, Mr...?"

"Stallion. Mark Stallion," the man answered, only a touch flustered by her contentious tone. He composed himself quickly, a wide smile filling his dark face. "My brother Luke said you'd be able to look over my bike for me. I'm headed to South Carolina and I just wanted to make sure she's road ready."

Michelle lifted her eyebrows, her head bobbing up and down ever so slightly. Her disposition softened ever so slightly. "So, you're one of Luke's brothers. How is he? I haven't heard from him in a while."

Mark shrugged. "He's well. How do you two know each other?" he asked curiously.

Michelle smiled, her eyes shimmering beneath the room's dim lights. She didn't bother to answer his question as she made her way from behind the counter to his side. As she paused in front of him, the top of her head barely reaching his chin, the light fragrance of a floral perfume mixed with a hint of motor oil teased his nostrils. Mark took a deep inhale, filling his lungs with the scent of her. He suddenly felt drunk with longing, the woman's imposing stare, commanding demeanor and gorgeous smile taking control of his senses. The feeling was unsettling, leaving Mark speechless.

"Roll your bike into the garage. The third bay. I'll get you on the road in no time," Michelle said, gesturing toward the work area.

Nodding, Mark moved toward the exit. Tossing a quick look back over his shoulder, he couldn't miss Michelle staring after him. He also didn't miss the fact that she'd not bothered to respond to his question and now his curiosity was seriously heightened. He couldn't wait to talk to his little brother to find out what was up with him and that woman.

Chapter 2

Myrtle Beach, North Carolina, was hot and Mark wasn't thinking about the ninety-plus-degree weather as he rolled up in front of Bimini's Oyster Bar and Seafood Café. The restaurant was one of his favorite haunts when he was in the area and he'd been thinking about their conch fritters since he'd crossed the border out of Georgia.

As he swung his large body off his vehicle, loosening the strap to his helmet, a group of scantily clad women caught his eye, the trio eyeing him hungrily. The bike event had no shortage of half-dressed females in want of attention, and Mark had always been amazed by how brazen some of them could be. Just that morning a buxom sister with platinum-blond braids in a string bikini that was more string than swimsuit had climbed right onto the back of his motorcycle, grabbing his crotch firmly as she'd whispered a proposition into his ear.

Mark had to admit the offer had been tempting, but he'd

politely turned her down, removing her grip from the front of his denim jeans as he'd sent her in the other direction. He shook his head at the memory then turned his attention back to his bike, not even bothering to acknowledge the three young women who were shaking their goodies for his attention. It suddenly dawned on him that he hadn't sought out any female companionship since his arrival. He pulled the back of his hand to his forehead to check if he might be running a temperature, certain that he had to have a fever.

His thoughts were interrupted by a slap on his shoulder, his attention turning to his good friend and riding buddy, Vanessa Long, who greeted him cheerily. Vanessa was waving her head from side to side, her caramel-colored eyes bulging at the wealth of eye candy that she found so tempting.

"Did you see the bootie on that babe? Her mama sure 'nuf blessed her!" the woman exclaimed excitedly.

Mark laughed. "Down girl! You're about to hurt yourself."

Vanessa laughed with him. "Yes, I am and I'm going to enjoy every second of the pain."

"Where'd you disappear to?" Mark asked as he secured his belongings in the side satchel on his bike. "One minute you were riding beside me and the next minute you were gone," he said as he and his friend made their way toward the restaurant's front entrance.

Vanessa grinned sheepishly. "Had to partake in some V-Twin foreplay," the woman said with a laugh.

Mark winced, shaking his head from side to side. He held up his hands in surrender. "Stop. Don't tell me any more," he said jokingly.

Vanessa laughed. "I met me a new friend from Florida. Baby girl likes a Harley so we rode up a steep hill, I shifted into low and the rest is history."

Mark laughed with her. He and Vanessa had grown up together, best friends since they'd met in elementary school. Vanessa had been all tomboy and her daredevil antics had rivaled his own, making their friendship a nice match. For a brief stint in high school they'd been boyfriend and girlfriend, the passion in their relationship never amounting to much of anything. Then in college Vanessa had admitted her predilection for women, turning their friendly rivalry up two notches. Mark had only been slightly disturbed when the woman had begun to be open about her interests. Interests that ran the same line as his. But over time they'd found their balance, Vanessa acting as if she were just one of the boys and he and his brothers treating her as such.

Inside the restaurant a young waiter with a short, blond bowl cut guided the duo to a booth as he handed them menus, promising to be right back with the two Heineken beers they ordered.

"This truly has been one good time," Vanessa exclaimed as they settled down for a relaxing lunch.

"Always is," Mark said, nodding his agreement. "There's nothing like it."

Both sat in deep reflection, thinking about the tons of parties and events that typically occurred throughout the five-day weekend. Revelers packed the hotels, the beaches were swamped, the streets packed with bikes and cars, and no matter where you were you could smell the barbecue grilling. In all of his travels, Mark hadn't found another party quite like it.

"So, how's the new bike handling?" Vanessa asked, lifting her cold bottle of brew to her thin lips.

Mark nodded. "She's been sweet," he answered, thoughts of his encounter with Michelle Coleman rising to the forefront of his mind. "The mechanic did a nice job," he added.

Vanessa nodded, her eyes sweeping around the room. "So where did Luke find this guy? I might need to take my ride there for some work."

Mark grinned. "That *guy*," he said, "isn't a guy." He recalled Michelle's admonishment when he'd referred to her as a girl. "She's a very attractive woman," he said, thoughts of the beauty wafting through his memory.

It had taken her less than an hour to give his bike a once-over before declaring it more than road ready for his journey. She'd given him a list of things to keep an eye on, detailing specifics he should do if he encountered any problems. Then she'd declared her services on the house, repayment of a favor his brother Luke had performed for her. He'd mustered up an apology for the *girl* faux pas and Michelle had given him a high-voltage smile that had highlighted brilliant pearl-white teeth for his efforts. He'd laughed warmly when she'd warned him not to let it happen again, dismissing him and crawling beneath the front end of a car that looked like it had seen many a better day.

Mark had been tempted to ask her to ride with him, to forgo his trip so he could take her to dinner, but she hadn't bothered to even look back in his direction. For the first time since forever Mark had exited a room wondering if he'd managed to leave any kind of an impression on a woman who had clearly left one on him.

Vanessa leaned forward in her seat, eyeing him curiously. "Just how attractive is attractive?" the woman asked, sensing a swift change in Mark's mood.

Blowing a deep exhalation of air, Mark turned his attention back to his friend, shrugging his broad shoulders. A wide grin filled his face. "Don't start. You're always trying to make something out of nothing."

Vanessa chuckled. "See, you left yourself open for that," she responded. "Your voice changed, you got this goofy look on your face, and you suddenly stopped talking so I know you had to be thinking something you weren't sharing."

Mark realized that there was some truth to what the woman had just said. He wasn't interested in sharing what little he knew about Michelle with anyone, most especially Vanessa with her meddlesome ways. He shook his head from side to side, ignoring Vanessa's comments as he changed the subject. When he was satisfied that Vanessa was focused on something other than his encounter with Michelle Coleman, he sighed, sipping at his own cool brew.

Soon, Vanessa was lauding the assets of a group of women who occupied a table near theirs. As he turned to gaze in the direction where his friend stared, the man couldn't help but think that not one of the women vying for some attention could hold a candle to the mechanic everyone called Mitch.

Michelle sat curled up in the window seat of her small townhome, staring out to the courtyard below. The sun had just begun to set and she was watching as her neighbors headed out for a night on the town. The woman in unit 2B actually had a date, a new face arriving in a freshly detailed Cadillac to escort her out. The newlyweds from 5D had left hand in hand, joy shimmering across their faces as they headed out.

Michelle sighed, not sure if she wanted to be depressed about not having a date on a Friday night or not. Getting a date wouldn't have been a problem—a long list of suitors continually vyed for her attention—but Mitch wasn't interested in spending time with any of the men who seemed to always be chasing after her.

Thoughts of Mark Stallion suddenly surfaced, causing a mild current of electricity to race up her spine. Their brief encounter had left her curious, wondering if he was as interesting as she imagined him to be. Luke had always talked highly of him, forever praising the siblings he looked up to, and Michelle couldn't help but be moved by the man's adoration of them. Having no siblings of her own, she could only imagine that kind of attachment to any blood relative. Her uncle, who'd been married to her father's sister, was her only living family and even the bond that existed between them didn't match the one Luke shared with his family.

She and Luke had met his junior year at Texas Southern University. Michelle had been teaching a basic automotive course and Luke had been her star pupil. The young man had spent an inordinate amount of time learning the fundamentals of an automotive engine and not once had he made any kind of a play for Michelle. Not all of his classmates had been as considerate, a few taxing Michelle's last nerve. One in particular had become very problematic. A late-night encounter with the brute might have ended very differently if Luke hadn't been there to intervene on Michelle's behalf. The man had cornered her in a classroom, the moment just shy of being a crime and Michelle a victim if Luke hadn't arrived when he did. The two had bonded over cups of Starbucks coffee, becoming fast friends and Michelle felt indebted to him, never forgetting how grateful she had been for his help.

Michelle moved from the window seat to the desk in the corner of the room, booting up the laptop computer that sat on the polished surface. When she accessed the Google home page, she typed in the words *Stallion Enterprises*. Seconds later she was scanning a listing of some 338,000 entries. Selecting the corporation's official Web site, she clicked the page for the corporate biographies, reviewing the data on Mark Stallion. Michelle couldn't help but be impressed by his lengthy résumé of accomplishments. One entry in particular, describing his services to the state's foster-care system, was of much interest to her. Some thirty minutes later Michelle had read every detail written there about the Stallion family.

Moving back to the window, Michelle returned her attention to the parking lot and another car with another couple that was pulling out of a space. She cradled a lukewarm cup of tea between her small palms, heaving a low sigh. Her Friday nights were starting to get too lonely, she thought as she settled the cup against the top of the coffee table. Rising from her seat, she reached for a lightweight jacket. Searching for her keys, she was determined not to let loneliness get to her. With any luck she could be back in the garage and under the hood of her car long before depression had a chance to set in.

Chapter 3

Luke Stallion was seated in his brother's leather executive chair when Mark entered his office. The younger sibling was flipping through a pile of papers, a look of bewilderment painting his expression. Mark chuckled under his breath as he stood in the doorway, watching the young man try to make sense of the stack of business documents before him.

"Is it that bad?" Mark finally asked, breaking the silence.

Luke jumped in his seat, obviously startled from deep thoughts. "Hey! When did you get here?"

Mark laughed. "Not long. You looked like you were doing something important. I didn't want to interrupt you."

Luke shrugged, dropping the pile of reports back to the desktop as he rose. "It's the quarterly numbers for the entire corporation. John wants me to run an analysis on them. He says that if I understand the numbers, then I'll understand which strategies work for the company and which ones don't."

Mark laughed again, his head bobbing up and down. "It's not that bad. He made us all do it one time or another."

"Anyone heard from him?" Luke asked as Mark moved behind the desk to reclaim his seat.

His brother shook his head. "His wife took him away for a long weekend. No one *wants* to hear from him. Marah would hurt him if he tried to call and check up on business."

Luke chuckled. "I know that's right. So what have you been up to? No one heard from you this weekend."

"A group of us went up to Big Piney Creek and did some white-water rafting."

"You're at the bike festival one week, kayaking the next. You're living large, bro! And what's this I hear about the company sponsoring a drag-racing team that you're going to be driving for?"

Mark grinned. "Pretty slick idea, huh! I came up with that one myself."

Luke rolled his eyes skyward. "Like that wasn't hard to figure out. I'm just surprised that John approved it."

"He hasn't. At least, not yet. We didn't think we needed to bother him with the details."

Luke raised one eyebrow questioningly. "Who's we?"

"Me, Matthew, and now you. It's a unanimous decision."

Luke rolled his eyes a second time. "Thanks for letting me know that I approved."

"You're welcome."

"And Matthew went along with all of this?" Luke questioned, knowing the answer before his brother could get the words past his lips.

"Yep."

Luke crossed his arms over his chest. "Did you bribe him or was it blackmail?"

Mark chuckled. "You really have the wrong impression about me, little brother. Sometimes you just have to take advantage of those unexpected opportunities that drop into your lap."

"And what was the name of this unexpected opportunity?"

Mark laughed again. "Stacy something-or-other. Matthew sort of got himself tangled between her and her sister Taylor. See, what it is was…"

Luke held up a hand, stalling the tall tale he knew his brother was about to spin. "Spare me the details," he said with a wry laugh, his brother laughing with him.

"But a racing team's a pretty risky venture, isn't it? And I'm not just talking about the financial risk," Luke said.

Mark shrugged, his broad shoulders pushing up toward his earlobes. "Life's too short to waste sitting around. You need to come hang out with me for a while and enjoy it a little more."

"Life's too short to be taking any unnecessary chances with these here bones. I think I'll just stick to the safe sports. Chess, pool, bingo. Those are good enough for me."

Mark laughed loudly, the warmth of it reverberating around the room, his brother laughing with him. A thought suddenly flooded his mind. He leaned forward in his seat, his hands folded beneath his chin as he rested his elbows against the desktop. "Luke, I met your mechanic friend, Mitch. Why you been holding out on us, boy? What's up that you had to keep that woman a secret?"

Luke's grin widened. "No secrets here. There was nothing to tell. Michelle's just a friend I met in school."

"A good friend?"

"I like to think so."

"So you two have something going on?"

Luke laughed. "Why are you asking?"

Mark leaned back in his seat. "Just curious," he said, fighting to keep his face from showing any emotion.

"Uh-huh. Well, no, it's not like that between us. We hang out together every now and then but it's definitely nothing romantic."

"Was it ever?"

"No. Why? Are you interested?"

Mark shrugged, trying to be nonchalant. "She was *interesting*," he said, his eye flitting back and forth as he purposely avoided his brother's gaze. "I wouldn't mind getting to know her a little better."

Luke folded his arms over his chest, a raised eyebrow studying his brother carefully. Mark's reputation with women was scandalous. His love-'em-and-leave-'em attitude had left many a broken heart across the great state of Texas, the whole Eastern Seaboard and some international territories as well.

Luke shook his head from side to side. "Michelle's not that kind of girl."

"Why does it have to be like that?" Mark asked, his tone voicing his annoyance at his brother's presumptions. "I can't just get to know a nice girl?"

"I'm sure you've gotten to know a few of them. That's half your problem. Michelle deserves a nice guy and there ain't nothing nice about you, big brother."

Mark pretended to pout. "My feelings are hurt."

"I doubt it," Luke said.

"You don't give me any credit. John was just saying that I might meet me a nice girl like Marah and really start to think about settling down. Mitch might be that girl, but how will I know if you're going to stand in the way of my getting to know her and letting her get to know me? She might actually like me."

"She might and then again..." Luke's voice dropped off, his eyes rolling skyward as he teased his sibling.

Mark chuckled. "So, are you going to put in a good word for me or not?"

Moving toward the door, Luke said nothing. As he paused in the entrance, he turned back to face his brother. "I'll give it some thought and let you know," he said finally.

Mark chuckled again, lifting that stack of papers from the desktop. "Fine. Be like that," he said. "And here I was going to help you with your analysis." He held the documents out toward Luke.

"That is so like you," Luke said, taking the papers from his hand. "I should have known you'd resort to bribery," he teased.

Mark laughed. "Did it work?"

Luke laughed with him. "Oh, heck, yeah!"

"That's what I thought. So when do I get your girl's telephone number?"

Luke's eyes widened with amusement. "Did you get Marah's e-mail?"

Mark looked confused. "What does Marah have to do—"

"Did you get Marah's message about her meet and greet at the club?" Luke asked again, interrupting his brother.

Mark nodded. "Yeah. So?"

"Make sure you're there."

"Why?"

"Because Michelle will be. Then you can ask her for her telephone number yourself."

Mark stared at his brother thoughtfully, a bright smile warming his face. He pointed his index finger in the man's direction. "Now who's bribing who!" he exclaimed cheerfully.

Luke grinned back. "Now, about those numbers…"

It just might be a nice gig, Michelle thought to herself as she read the formal letter that had come to her via express mail. *Then again, maybe it wouldn't be.* She had purposely ignored the document at first but, Simon being Simon, he had pulled it from the trash bin where she'd thrown it and had waved it wildly for her attention.

Michelle read the details for the hundredth time, her emotions waffling back and forth as she mulled over the possibilities. Had she even anticipated this happening to her when she'd gotten up that morning she would have rolled back under the covers and stayed there. She hadn't been at all prepared for the business opportunity that happenstance had just afforded her.

It wasn't every day that a woman was offered the position of head mechanic for a NHRA Pro Stock motorcycle team and Michelle could now say that she'd not only been offered the position, but that the offer had come with an endorsement from a former president of the NHRA. Not bad for the little girl most thought would never find her way back to the racing tracks after her father's untimely death years earlier.

Michelle had been her father's protégée, Brent Mitchell Coleman teaching her everything about the mechanical operations of an engine. Michelle had doted on the man, following him around like a second shadow from the moment she could walk and talk. Her mother had disappeared from their lives before Michelle's fifth birthday and her father had become the center of her world.

As a little girl, a garage had been Michelle's playground, pneumatic air tools the toys she played with. By the time she was sixteen years old Michelle could overhaul an automobile engine like a seasoned professional, her skills outranking those of many grown men.

Over the years her father had raced anything on wheels but motorcycles had been his first love. Michelle remembered

well the day her father had received his own formal invita-
tional letter to drive a bike for one of the most prestigious Pro
Stock motorcycle teams in competition. The two had celebrated with a large pepperoni pizza and ice cold bottles of
Corona beer.

Both Michelle and Simon had been a part of the pit crew,
maintaining her father's bike and keeping him on track.
The accident had been a fluke of sorts, coming just before
one of the largest national races. The win would have
ranked her father as the number one seeded driver in the
nation and Michelle had been sure he would win. Instead,
the fatal crash had ended all of their dreams and left
Michelle completely devastated. She was still haunted by
the memory of the brake line that was found mysteriously
severed. The formal investigation had ruled it an accident,
but Michelle had always been convinced that accidents like
that didn't just happen without a little outside help. She still
blamed herself for not double-checking her father's bike
one last time.

Michelle heaved a deep sigh, folding the formal document
back into the legal-size envelope it had been delivered in.
Tossing it back on the counter, she returned to the inventory
she'd been taking, her focus on the box of gaskets and pipes
she'd been counting.

Simon was still eyeing her from across the room, waiting
hopefully for a reaction that he knew Michelle wasn't going
to show. Never one to be outwardly demonstrative, they'd all
grown used to Michelle's passive demeanor, the expression-
less eyes that never gave a hint to her feelings. Simon knew
that Michelle wouldn't let him know if she were interested in
the job or not until she was on the payroll. But he was excited
for her and didn't mind letting her know. The young woman's

career was definitely on target as far as he was concerned. Now, if they could only do something about her personal life.

Booting up the computer on his desk, Mark had more on his mind than he cared to have. There was a pile of client portfolios on his desk screaming for his attention. Half his day had already been shot to hell haggling with his younger brother, and thoughts of that woman kept creeping into his mind. That woman. Mark's body quivered at the thought of Michelle, the cool chill racing the length of his spine having become too familiar since the two had met.

Mark was finding it difficult to rationalize what was happening to him. Never before had a woman consumed his waking moments the way Michelle Coleman kept invading his mind. Most especially a woman he'd not even had an opportunity to take to dinner yet. For crying out loud, he thought to himself, shifting in his seat. The two had only met for five short minutes, the woman barely giving him a second look. He couldn't begin to believe how love struck he was suddenly acting.

The man shook his head vigorously to dislodge the images of Michelle from his mind. Fighting to refocus, he scanned his to-do list for the umpteenth time. At the rate things were going, he thought, the rest of his day couldn't get any worse because things were already bad enough.

He turned his attention back to the folders before him, flipping through them casually before finally tossing his hands in the air in frustration. He was glad John was not around to give him hell for slacking off on the job. John was a true tyrant when it came to business. Typically, he was, too, but on this particular day, Mark was lacking that kind of fortitude.

If the truth were to be told, when he wasn't thinking about Michelle, he was anxious to get down to the new athletic facility that housed Stallion Racing. The ten-bay garage had quickly become his favorite place, his home away from home as he maneuvered his way around the mechanics of the new Kawasaki motorcycles that they had recently acquired. He was anxious to get out to the track to give one a test spin around the blacktop. He was missing the squeal of brakes and the smell of burning rubber and just the thought was making him more antsy with each passing moment. He was past ready to get out of the office and the Armani suit that he swore was cutting off his circulation. But those darn folders and the documents inside would not allow him to leave.

An hour or so later his secretary buzzed for his attention. "Mr. Stallion?"

"Yes, Elena," Mark replied, depressing the response button on the intercom.

"Vanessa Long is on line two, sir. She's returning your call."

"Thank you," Mark said as Elena disconnected the speaker. He depressed the button flashing up at him. "Hey, girl! What's up?" Mark chimed cheerily.

"Not much, my friend. How are things with you?" Vanessa responded.

"Woman, it's been one of those days," he answered, chuckling under his breath. "So, how's that new business venture starting out?" Mark asked, alluding to the new sales opportunities Vanessa had spoken about in Myrtle Beach. "You wheeling and dealing with the big boys yet?"

"Oh, yeah!" Vanessa hummed cheerily. "I'm wheeling all right. You'd be surprised what these fools will buy if they think they can get a little something-something on the side."

Mark laughed with her. "Did you tell them your something-something is very selective?"

"Oh, I made sure they knew how selective it is, honey.

Makes them want me even more, but there is absolutely no testosterone allowed on these premises."

"Okay, there now," Mark said, grimacing slightly. "Let's change the subject. So what can I do for you today?"

"You called me, remember? I just got your message and was returning your call," Vanessa said. "I think the bigger question is what can I do for you?"

Mark nodded, suddenly remembering why it was he'd called his friend in the first place. "I need an escort Friday night. Are you available?"

"Oh," Vanessa chimed. "Black tie, I hope? I need a reason to get all dolled up."

"Hardly, more like business chic," Mark said, his tone denoting little interest. "It's for some meet and greet thing my sister-in-law is hosting for her business. You remember Marah's sister Eden, right? You met her at John and Marah's wedding," Mark continued, not bothering to wait for Vanessa to respond. "Well, she and Marah own that new dating service downtown. I promised I'd stop by, but I figured I might need a quick exit. Just in case. You know?"

Vanessa chuckled. "Not interested in greeting and meeting some new women? Sounds like it would be a really good time to me."

Mark shook his head from side to side, oblivious to the fact that his friend couldn't see him. He wasn't interested in meeting any new women. He was only interested in meeting one woman. He was anxious for an opportunity to be in the room with his new favorite female mechanic again. But he couldn't tell Vanessa that and so he denied having any interest at all. "You would think so. Personally, I'm not in the mood to be stuck in a room with a bunch of desperate women looking for a man."

"They're not all desperate for a man now," Vanessa said with a wry laugh.

Mark groaned. "Spare me, please. Do you want to go or not? You know the routine. I need a back door out just in case."

Vanessa laughed. "Am I the girlfriend or the wife?"

"Whatever it takes to get me out of any bad situations quick."

"I guess I can do that. Since we're such good friends and all."

"I got your good friend," Mark laughed.

"Are you buying dinner, too? This really sounds like it would call for a good steak dinner afterward."

"I swear, Vanessa. For a woman who has never officially dated me, you surely are expensive."

"I take that as a yes," Vanessa said sweetly.

Mark groaned. "Just meet me there at seven o'clock on Friday and we'll go from there. The place is called the Post Club. I'll keep my eye out for you."

"I'm sure I'll have no problems finding it. I'll talk to you later," Vanessa said.

"Yeah, later," Mark said as he disconnected the call. And then, for just a brief moment, he couldn't help but wonder if inviting Vanessa might have actually been a bad idea after all.

Chapter 4

Matthew Stallion pulled his silver BMW into the driveway of Briscoe Ranch. Mark rode shotgun and baby brother Luke took up the backseat. All three men were excited to be spending their day away from the office and out in the field. Briscoe Ranch had become John and Marah's homestead, the family acreage bequeathed to them on the day of their wedding by her father, Edward Briscoe. Briscoe Ranch was well over eight hundred acres of working cattle ranch and an equestrian center, and its daily operations now fell under the umbrella of Stallion Enterprises' responsibilities. It had been the compromise that had eventually sealed the deal on an acquisition that had proved to be a challenge to the four Stallion brothers.

Back in the day, Marah's father, Edward Briscoe, had been one of the original black cowboys, he and his first wife expanding the Texas longhorn operation to include an entertainment complex that specialized in corporate and private client services. The ranch now housed two twenty-thousand-square-foot event barns, and a country bed-and-breakfast. With the property being central to Austin, Houston, Dallas and Fort Worth, Briscoe Ranch had soon made quite a name for itself.

Just weeks before John and Marah's wedding, patriarch Edward had married Juanita, the Stallion family's surrogate mother. The two families had merged nicely together and with the two marriages came the acquisition of the ranch and all it had to offer. All the Stallion men were excited about the challenge to expand this area of their business, wanting to build a world-renowned equestrian facility known for its community outreach programs. Each of them was committed to affording young boys and girls from impoverished homes the experience of ranch life up close and personal. Mark, in particular, had made it his personal pet project.

As the three men made their way up the steps of the oversize home, Juanita greeted them at the door, her excitement uncontained. The petite woman reached to wrap her arms tightly around thick necks.

"Oh, how I've missed you boys!" Juanita exclaimed, her gray hair swaying down against her shoulders.

"You need to come into the office more often to see us, Aunt Juanita," Mark said as he lifted her from the ground in a deep bear hug.

"Soon. I promise," Juanita answered. "There's been so much going on here that I've just had my hands full." She gestured for them to follow her. "Come on in. We were all getting breakfast," she said softly.

Inside the large home, the rest of the Briscoe-Stallion clan were gathered around the kitchen island consuming a home-cooked meal. The men were greeted by the delectable aroma of pan-fried potatoes, thick sausage and seasoned eggs.

"Looks like we're just in time," Matthew said, reaching for an empty plate off the counter. "Good morning, everyone."

"Good morning," said Edward and his daughters, Marah and Eden.

"There are homemade biscuits in the oven," Marah's twin sister Marla said, her infant son looking curiously about from her lap.

Mark grinned. "No wonder our big brother can't ever be found. A beautiful wife and homemade biscuits, too! You've got it made, boy!" he exclaimed, slapping John on the back.

"I go away for a few days and now I can't be found." John rolled his eyes skyward as he pulled another forkful of potatoes into his mouth. "Please."

Luke laughed. "Please nothing. Before, you would take a vacation and we'd hear from you every day. When's the last time you talked to him, Matt?"

Matthew shook his head. "He didn't call me."

"Me either," Mark chuckled.

Marah grinned widely, moving to wrap her arms around her husband's neck. "A good woman will do that for you. You boys should try it one day," she said as she planted a kiss against John's cheek.

John's smile was even wider than hers. "Don't be jealous, boys," he said as he hugged Marah tightly.

They all laughed, chattering easily together as they consumed their morning meal.

"You all are coming to our event tonight, aren't you?" Eden asked, looking from one brother to the others.

Luke nodded eagerly. "And, I'm bringing a good friend. You remember Michelle, don't you, Marah?"

Marah nodded. "Oh, I really liked her. I'm glad she's coming. I know just the men to introduce her to."

Mark bristled ever so slightly. "Maybe she doesn't want to be introduced to any men," he said, his eyes shifting across his plate as he tried to avoid Marah's curious stare.

Luke eyed Marah and chuckled. "But that's why she's coming, Mark. I told her if anyone can help her find a good man that Marah can."

Mark raised one eyebrow, lifting his gaze slightly to meet his brother's. "Did you now?" he asked, his tone voicing his displeasure at the sudden thought of his favorite mechanic meeting any other men.

Luke laughed out loud. John looked from Mark to Luke and back again, cutting his gaze toward Matthew. "Did I miss something?"

Matthew shrugged. "Beats me."

Mark frowned. "No, you didn't miss a thing. Your brother just thinks he's funny, that's all."

Luke laughed again, shaking his head vigorously.

Marah interjected. "Well, just so you're prepared, Mark. I think it would be nice if you got to know Michelle better. Unless of course you think Matt would be a better choice for her?"

Mark cast his gaze toward Marah, a rush of heat warming his cheeks as he shook his head vehemently. He stammered, choking on a piece of food. Juanita rushed to his aid, the small of her palm hammering against his broad back.

"I swear, Mark," Juanita exclaimed. "It doesn't take a rocket scientist to see that you're obviously interested in this girl."

Edward shook his head. "Son, I think Juanita done peeped your hold card!"

Mark tapped a closed fist against his chest as he gasped for air. Everyone around him was laughing heartily.

"You all leave Mark be," Juanita said warmly, her gaze glistening with joy. "Y'all gone make him jump scared before he gets a chance to know the girl."

Luke grinned, reaching for another biscuit. "Not me, Aunt Juanita. I've got a bet riding on this meeting. And I don't like to lose."

It was a nice crowd, Mark thought to himself. A very nice group of current clients, former customers and newbies interested in the services the Post Club might have to offer filled the room. Mark watched as Marah and Eden worked the room. They'd been going strong for well over an hour as they guided singles into groups and groups into couples. As he looked anxiously toward the door for the umpteenth time, he noted the arrival of his brothers as Luke and John entered the room at the same time. Luke's friend Michelle was nowhere to be found.

Marah rushed to greet them, wrapping both men in a deep hug. "This is so exciting!" she gushed, her gaze racing around the perimeter of the room. "We've had a great turnout tonight."

John nodded his head, looking from one sister to the other. "It looks like you and Eden have done a great job," he said as he leaned his six-foot-plus frame down to kiss her cheek. "Congratulations, baby," he said, hugging her tightly against his solid body.

"Thank you," Marah said excitedly.

"Is Michelle still coming?" Mark asked, moving to join the trio. His attention fell on Luke's face, eagerness flooding his expression. He glanced toward the door one more time.

"Hello to you, too," John said, rolling his eyes skyward.

Luke echoed his sentiments. "Boy, is that how you greet your family?"

"Hey," Mark said with a quick nod. "So, is she?"

Before Luke could respond, the entrance door opening and

then closing pulled at their attention. The small group turned at the same time to see who was coming through the doorway. Mark was suddenly taken aback as he caught sight of the exquisite woman making her entrance.

"Hot damn!" Mark exclaimed under his breath, his eyes widening with excitement.

Donning a silk dress that was the color of summer-kissed peaches, Michelle surveyed the room in search of a familiar face. The woman cleaned up nicely, Mark thought, admiring the formfitting dress that hugged her lean body. Michelle was long and slender with more leg than torso and the length of her legs was displayed boldly from ankle to upper thigh. Mark's gaze raced the length of her body, taking in every taut muscle he and everyone else was privy to see.

The moderate length of her hair was cut in a neat bob, the silken strands barely brushing against her shoulders and her chiseled features were perfection personified. Michelle was so beautiful he thought she could have easily rivaled any top model maneuvering a Parisian catwalk. Mark found himself tongue-tied when Luke called out Michelle's name. He watched as his brother excused himself and then headed in the direction of the door.

Marah tossed a look in Mark's direction then turned her attention back to Luke and Michelle as they stopped to greet each other with a warm embrace. She leaned into her husband's side, whispering softly as she glanced up at him. "I think this is going to be the easiest love connection I've ever made," she said with a low giggle.

John laughed with her. "Sorry to disappoint you, baby doll, but I think this connection was made well before you," he said, eyeing his brother curiously as Mark continued to stare at Michelle.

Marah giggled. "I hate to agree, honey, but I think you're right," she said, watching as her brother-in-law stood oblivious beside them.

Still standing in the entrance, Michelle was suddenly aware that she was being admired, Mark's gaze burning hot in her direction. She met his stare with one of her own, her palms running the short length of her silk dress as she moistened her lips. Beside her, Luke was chatting eagerly, but Michelle didn't have a clue what he was saying, his words lost as her attention was diverted elsewhere.

Mark stood well over six feet tall, his solid frame strong and sturdy. His complexion was Hershey's chocolate dark, richly decadent and teasing to the senses. His thick dreadlocks hung down his back, framing the lines of his face like the majestic mane on a lion. Dressed in a classic, charcoal Armani suit, his smoldering bedroom eyes and engaging, enigmatic smile had Michelle's full attention.

The man gestured with his head, every ounce of his body language welcoming her into the room. Nodding slowly, Michelle took in the sculpted features of the man's face. Mark Stallion was drop-dead gorgeous. She found herself staring at the curl of his full lips as he grinned at her, unable to stop herself from wondering what it might be like to kiss the lush pillows. She had to force her attention back to his eyes, shaking the clouds of fantasy that had suddenly washed over her.

Before Michelle realized what was happening, Luke had her by the elbow, guiding her in the direction of his brother and the gaze that suddenly had her weak in the knees. When they were standing side by side, everyone smiling widely, Luke made the introductions. "John, Marah, you remember my friend, Mitch, don't you? Mitch, this is my oldest brother John and his wife, Marah. Marah and her sister are our hosts for the evening."

Michelle nodded her head, extending her hand in greeting. "It's very nice to see you both again," she said softly.

"It's very nice to see you again as well," John responded.

"We're glad you could join us," Marah added.

Luke gestured toward his other brother. "And I think you've met my brother Mark."

Michelle nodded, her eyes locking with Mark's. The man's gaze was still blistering, his excitement shimmering like a raging fire from his dark eyes.

"We did. How are you?" Michelle said, her smile warming the contours of her face. She extended her hand toward his.

"I'm very well, thank you," Mark said, squeezing her fingers noticeably between his own. "It's really good to see you again."

Michelle smiled widely, the warmth of the gesture flooding her face. She suddenly felt herself blushing, a wave of color rising to her cheeks. She pulled her fingers from beneath Mark's, drawing her palm against her abdomen to stall the quiver of muscle that had her shaking. Drawing in a deep breath, it took everything within her to keep standing on her quivering knees. There was a shared current of electricity that passed between them. The energy was so palpable that everyone around them could feel it. The moment was interrupted as Luke told the story of how he and Michelle had come to be friends.

"My goodness," Marah exclaimed. "What a blessing it is that neither one of you was injured. Anything could have happened!"

Michelle nodded. "I'm grateful that Luke arrived when he did."

Marah nodded her agreement. "Well, Mitch, we're just delighted that you could join us this evening. Can I get you something to drink? Eat?"

Michelle shook her head. "Nothing, thank you. I didn't mean to crash your party like this, but Luke insisted that I meet him here."

"You're not crashing at all," Marah said, her gaze sweeping up to her husband's. "We're delighted that you could join us and I hope that you enjoy yourself. You might want to take advantage of some of our services," she said, sliding into her salesperson tone. "Then again," she continued as her eyes met Mark's, "maybe you don't need them."

Michelle responded with a smile.

John's eyes met Mark's stare, Mark still looking at Michelle with longing. "If you and Mitch will excuse us, please. I need to steal my woman away for a moment," John said, clasping his fingers between Marah's. Marah gave Michelle and Mark a wink as she followed her husband.

Mark nodded, suddenly feeling nervous. The rise of anxiety intensified as Luke excused himself as well, leaving him and Mitch alone together. There was a moment of awkward silence that suddenly filled the space between them.

"So, Mr. Stallion, how was your trip to the beach?" Michelle asked, moving to ease the rise of tension between them.

He nodded. "It was great. The bike rode like a dream. And please, call me Mark."

Michelle nodded ever so slightly. "Well, Mark, do you come to many of these things?" she asked, glancing around the room.

Mark shook his head. "This is my first and I'm only here because Marah insisted."

Michelle raised one eyebrow, eyeing him curiously. "That's the only reason?"

The man smiled shyly. "I'm not big on these kinds of things."

"But you might meet someone special," Michelle said, a coquettish aura washing over her expression.

Mark resisted the sudden urge to take a step closer to her, the sweet scent of her perfume rising like a warm mist around them. *I already have,* he thought to himself, fighting not to say the words out loud. Instead he said, "I might," his voice seeming to drop an octave. "I guess if you're single you can always use a little help with finding romance. Don't you agree?"

Michelle nodded. "I do, but I imagine you've got plenty of game when it comes to dealing with women."

"Oh, I've got game," Mark said with a soft chuckle. "I've got great game. My problem is I keep losing the game."

Michelle laughed with him. 'Well, that's not a good thing."

"No, it isn't."

The noise level in the room seemed to rise an octave as they stood in discussion. Mark suddenly wanted Michelle all to himself as they continued their conversation, oblivious to everyone else around them. He gestured for her to follow as he headed in the direction of Marah's office, leaving the noise and laughter of the crowd behind them.

"That's better," Mark said as he closed the door to the inner sanctuary. "I can hear myself think now."

"It did start to get a little noisy in there," Michelle answered.

Mark smiled as he leaned back against the large wooden desk that sat room center. Resting against the edge, he crossed his arms over his chest, trying not to appear as anxious as he felt.

"So, tell me more about this race team," Michelle said, eyeing him curiously.

Mark shrugged his broad shoulders. "I'm looking forward to the upcoming time trials. I think my team will do very well this season. This project is my baby and I'm out to prove myself."

"Have you been racing long?"

"A few years now. How about you? I know you can fix 'em but do you ride as well?"

Michelle nodded. "I don't race but I learned to ride before I learned to walk. My father drove for Rockman Racing."

A look of surprise crossed Mark's face. "Really? Who was your father?"

Michelle paused briefly before answering. "Brent Coleman."

There was a moment of recognition, the stories of Brent Coleman's demise washing over Mark's face. "I didn't know," he said softly, suddenly embarrassed. "My condolences for your loss."

Michelle gave him a quick smile. "Thank you. And it's okay. I don't mind talking about my father."

"I understand. I lost both my parents in an automobile accident when I was very young so I know what that's like."

Michelle was staring at him with glazed eyes. Her stare seemed to gently caress Mark's face. "I'm sorry. I didn't know."

Mark shrugged. "Let's change the subject. So, what do you do in your free time?"

"Repair engines," Michelle answered with a low chuckle.

Mark laughed as well. "Okay, but I'm sure you entertain yourself with other things as well."

The young woman nodded. "I do. I love anything that gives me an adrenaline rush, and engines give me one heck of a rush!"

Mark nodded slowly, his eyebrows raised ever so slightly.

Michelle laughed. "Strap one onto your back and I'll show you what I mean," she said, the words slipping out of her mouth before she could catch them.

Mark roared, mirth spilling between them like water from a faucet.

A wave of silence washed over the two of them as both gathered their thoughts, thoroughly enjoying the moment and the company. Michelle heaved a low sigh, color flooding her cheeks.

"Are you okay?" Mark asked.

Her head bobbed slightly. "This might be a little forward, Mark, but are you involved with anyone?" she asked, staring into his eyes.

He shook his head, his eyes widening brightly. "No, I'm not. Are you?" he asked, finally taking that step toward her.

The two were suddenly so close that Michelle could feel the heat from his body melting into her own. The power of the moment seemed to surface with a vengeance, taking full control. The rise in temperature was consuming, perspiration beading from her pores. Before she could catch herself, she'd pressed the length of her manicured fingers against his chest, the beat of his heart pulsating against her palm. As she lifted her eyes to meet his, Mark pressed one palm against the back of her hand and the other around her waist, drawing Michelle closer to him.

Before either could utter another word, the office door swung open, Marah and her sister rushing in from the other side. Both Marah and Eden looked from one to the other, concern filling their faces. Behind them, Luke was shaking his head anxiously. Michelle felt as if she'd been caught with her hands in the cookie jar, and a wave of embarrassment swept over her.

Mark took two quick steps back, his cheeks heated with color. When he caught sight of the young woman following on Marah's heels, his expression dropped straight to the floor.

Marah spoke first. "Mark, we found you," she said, her churlish tone causing him to cringe.

He nodded, trying to mask his discomfort. "Mitch and I were just talking," he said anxiously, his gaze sweeping from one face to another.

The woman behind Marah pushed her way forward, moving

to the front of the crowd. She extended her hand in Michelle's direction. "Hello, I'm Vanessa Long. Mark's fiancée."

Michelle shot Mark a quick look then stared back as Marah finished the introductions.

"Vanessa, this is Michelle Coleman, a close friend of Luke's."

The other woman gushed politely. "It's so nice to meet you." She looped an arm through Mark's, reaching up to kiss his cheek. "Hi, honey. I told you I'd make it!"

Chapter 5

"Men make me sick," Michelle muttered for the ump-teenth time. She kicked her high-heeled pumps from her size-seven feet as she settled the length of her body against a plush sofa.

"We're not all that bad," Simon offered, leaning the wealth of his weight against the back of the upholstered furniture. He gently massaged the young woman's shoulders, both staring in the direction of the flat-screen television playing with the volume turned down.

"In fact," the elderly man continued, "there are a few of us who are actually quite decent," he said matter-of-factly.

"Well, clearly there is nothing decent about Mark Stallion. The man lied," Michelle said, meeting her uncle's gaze. "He straight up lied to me. *No, I'm not involved with anyone,*" she said, mimicking Mark's comments. "So, what was that all about with him and his *fiancée?*"

Simon shrugged. "I couldn't tell you," he answered. "He didn't say anything else?"

"I didn't give him a chance. I was sure he was just going to tell some more lies so I walked out." She heaved a deep sigh.

Her uncle squeezed her shoulder gently. "I'm sorry, Mitch. I had really hoped you'd have a good time."

Michelle heaved another sigh, warm breath blowing past her lips into the air-conditioned room. "Liars and cheats," Michelle muttered. "All of 'em. Liars and cheats."

Simon chuckled. "Well, at least you found out before it went anywhere rather than afterward."

Michelle nodded in agreement. "He sure seemed like a great guy though, Uncle Simon," she said wistfully.

Simon stared down at her, the melancholy in her voice tugging at his heartstrings. He had a few choice words for that Stallion fellow. Simon didn't take kindly to anyone causing his surrogate daughter grief.

Michelle sighed again, suddenly feeling self-conscious at her behavior. She couldn't begin to explain why she'd reacted so strongly. It wasn't like there was anything between her and that man. The two barely knew each other, but she'd been excited at the prospect of getting to know him better. Mark Stallion had excited her and now she was reeling from the disappointment.

Rising from her seat, Michelle moved into the small galley kitchen, searching the contents of her freezer. Tucked out of sight behind a stack of frozen dinners and a foil-wrapped package she couldn't begin to identify was a pint of butter pecan ice cream. Pulling it and a spoon into her hands, Michelle returned to the television, dropping heavily back to her seat. Simon sat down beside her, and reached for the television remote that sat on the glass-topped end table.

"Put it on the *Speed Channel,*" Michelle said as she scooped the first spoonful of frozen dessert into her mouth.

Simon shook his head, a moment of confusion washing over his expression. "The *Speed Channel?*"

Michelle spooned a second taste of ice cream into her mouth. "NASCAR's on and, unlike most men, a good car race has never failed me."

Mark had been pacing the floor and ranting like a madman ever since Michelle had stormed out of Marah's office. The woman had barely bothered to say goodbye as she'd made her exit. He'd been stunned, unable to think straight as Vanessa had commanded everyone's full attention, feigning excitement about her fiancé Mark. The man heaved a deep sigh.

"It's your own fault," Luke admonished. "What were you thinking?"

"He wasn't thinking. That's half the problem," Marah said. "I thought you liked Mitch?"

"I did. I mean I do. I… It just…" Mark stammered, fumbling to form a complete sentence.

Vanessa laughed. "I don't know what you're getting all worked up about," she said, mirth gleaming in her pale eyes. "You told me you didn't want any attachments so what's the problem?"

Mark stopped in his tracks, doing an about-face to stare at his friend. "And did you have to keep going on and on? And where did you get that damn ring?"

Vanessa smiled, holding up the ring finger on her left hand and the four-carat cubic zirconia ring that adorned it. "Nice touch, huh?"

Mark rolled his eyes. "Well, if you had just shut up for two seconds I might have been able to explain."

John chuckled. "Not likely. I didn't get the impression that Mitch was hearing anything you had to say."

"And what about that?" Mark questioned, tossing his hands into the air. "Don't you think she overreacted?"

His big brother laughed. "I think you play too much. This is what happens when you play all the time."

Mark scowled, his expression showing his displeasure with his sibling's assessment.

Vanessa shrugged. "Well," she said nonchalantly, "it could have been worse. Just imagine if I had come as your pregnant wife!"

Mark woke early, no sign of morning light peeking through his bedroom windows. Opening his eyes, he struggled to focus then gave up, falling back against the mound of pillows as he closed his eyes tightly. His whole body felt as if he'd been run over by a Mack truck.

Taking a deep inhalation he blew stale breath past his full lips then rolled over onto his side. No one had answered the telephone number that Luke had given him for Michelle. Each time he'd dialed and the phone had rung, Mark imagined her purposely avoiding his calls, still believing he was engaged to be married to the likes of Vanessa. Even his little brother had not been able to get through to her to help pave the way to an explanation and an apology.

A wave of nausea rippled through Mark's abdomen. He wanted to be sick but he fought the vile sensation. His night hadn't gone at all the way he'd hoped. It had started on a grand high and then just like that the energy had deflated like a burst balloon gone awry.

His family had been less than sympathetic over his dilemma and his buddy Vanessa had been the only one to find any humor in the moment. Mark rolled over onto his stomach, pressing his abs, chest and face tight against the mattress.

Mark had no explanation for what he was feeling, but the past evening's events were weighing heavy on his spirit. It wasn't like this was the first time Vanessa had ever interceded on his behalf, saving him from what surely would have been a relationship disaster. And, if you had asked him before he'd met Michelle he would have told you that it wouldn't have been the last time. But something about the beguiling woman had him totally unsettled, spiraling so far off his game that he couldn't remember how to play.

It was way too early to call her, he thought as he lifted his body slightly to peer at the digital clock on the nightstand. Then again, he thought, what did he have to lose? Maybe he'd get lucky and catch her off guard. Maybe she'd have a change of heart and he'd be able to explain that it had all been one bad mix-up. Maybe Michelle would have found the funny that had kept Vanessa doubled over with laughter. As Mark reached for his cell phone and hit the redial button all he could think was *just maybe*.

Michelle wasn't happy and her vile mood was far from pleasant. She'd tossed and turned most of the night, sleeping coming in sporadic doses. When she'd finally been able to fall into a deep slumber, the ringing telephone had wakened her, leaving her wide-eyed and evil.

Caller ID had burst many a telemarketer's dreams but Michelle had been more than grateful for the little invention. Recognizing the familiar number had kept her from answering the early-morning call, insuring that her bad mood wasn't made worse with her cussing that man out.

She'd been very tempted to pick up the call and cuss.

Instead she'd disconnected the ringer on her telephone. Unable to fall back to sleep, she'd risen from her bed, had tossed on a pair of jeans and a sweatshirt and now she was standing in the center of the garage trying to decide which repair job she wanted to tackle first.

Michelle rested her hands against her lean hips. Thinking about Mark Stallion and why she was in the garage at five o'clock in the morning only served to make her angrier. But she was not going to be moved by the pretty, rich boy who thought the world revolved around him and him alone. Clearly the man had too much time on his hands if he was able to play the games he seemed to be playing with her. As far as Michelle was concerned, Mark Stallion could call all he wanted. She had no intentions of ever answering.

Chapter 6

"Do the words *big* and *baby* mean anything to you?" Vanessa asked, her hands hinged to the shelves of her full hips.

"What are you trying to say?" Mark answered, tinkering with the engine of his new race bike.

"I'm not trying to say anything. I said what I had to say. You're acting like a *big baby*. What's with you?"

The man rolled his eyes, not bothering to respond. Instead, he straddled his bike, turned the ignition and backed the bike out of the garage. Vanessa walked out behind him, leaning against the railing as he made his way onto the racetrack. Three laps around the paved surface and Mark was suddenly feeling more like himself. By lap twenty, he was a changed man. Vanessa noted the immediate difference in his attitude.

"Feeling better?" she asked as he swung off his bike, removing his helmet from his head.

Mark nodded, shrugging his shoulders. "Much. Sorry

about before but you know…" His voice trailed off as he cut his eye in her direction and back out to the track.

Vanessa nodded. "So am I. I didn't mean to mess up what you had going on. I just figured…well…you know…" She paused as well, knowing that Mark would be able to finish her thought without her saying another word.

Mark extended a closed fist and Vanessa punched back. "It's cool," he said. "I'm over it."

She smiled. "So—" She was interrupted by the loud roar of a Suzuki race bike careening around the track. Both of them turned to stare, captivated by the precision machinery that was taking the curves with ease. The driver was leaning so sharply that the bike practically lay on its side, both driver and machine appearing as though they might fall flat at any moment.

So enthralled were the two of them watching that neither noticed that they were not alone. A rotund man with a Santa beard and mustache had moved to their side and was watching just as intently, his hands pushed deep into the pockets of his khaki slacks. His head was bobbing up and down against his shoulders in excitement and it was only when he let out a very loud whoop did they realize he was there.

Vanessa jumped, startled only momentarily. Mark turned about suddenly, and then greeted the man with cool acknowledgment. "Greg Rockman. Why am I not surprised to run into you?" Mark asked, his tone chilly.

The Santa impersonator grinned broadly. "It's nice to see you as well, Stallion. How might you be this fine afternoon?"

Mark nodded. "I'm doing quite well, thank you for asking. I was just telling my friend here that I'm looking forward to wiping up the track with your boys this season. Things couldn't be looking better if you were to ask me."

Vanessa watched with amusement, leaning with her back

against the fence that separated them from the racecourse. She looked back and forth from one man to the other, clearly entertained at the exchange. Few knew that Greg Rockman was not one of Mark's favorite people, something about the man's business practices not sitting well with her friend. When it was necessary, Mark was very good at masking his distaste for the man but Vanessa knew it wouldn't be but so long before her friend would be ready to drop his cordial facade.

Rockman smiled a wide grin that stretched from ear to ear. "I'm sure you're going to give it your best shot," the man answered, turning his attention back to the bike and the driver. "But I don't think," he continued, his tone smug, "that you'll be wiping up much with the team I've put together. We've got a secret weapon this year that's going to make all you boys wish you'd stayed home where you couldn't get your feelings hurt."

Vanessa wouldn't have thought it possible but the man's smile widened even further, his whole body quivering like a bowl of cherry Jell-O as he chuckled.

Mark gave him a wry smile back. "And what's this secret weapon you're so proud of?"

"Now, it wouldn't be a secret if I told you, would it?"

Mark rolled his eyes, turning back to stare where the other man stared. The driver was slowing down, taking the bike around with a lazy ease. Mark wasn't quite sure if there was something wrong with the vehicle or if the driver had just grown weary of the exhilaration. He was suddenly surprised when Rockman gestured for the driver to join them, the man waving excitedly for attention. "That's one of yours?" Mark asked casually.

"That's what's going to whip your tail this season."

Mark cut his eye at the man and back to the bike and driver that was headed in their direction.

* * *

Easing the bike forward, Michelle was only so surprised to see her new employer standing side by side with Mark Stallion. She'd known that once she accepted the position it would only have been matter of time before she and that man would run into each other. If Michelle were completely honest, Mark Stallion had motivated her to accept the position with his opposition. Michelle was looking forward to beating Stallion at one of his games. Once she'd said yes, running into him had been inevitable. But it had to be some kind of bad karma for it to have happened on her first day on the job.

Coming to a complete stop, she shut down the engine and lifted herself from the bike, setting it back against the kickstand. Reaching for the strap on her helmet, she was focused on the tall black man who was studying her curiously. He was even more beautiful than she'd remembered, she thought to herself. Her stomach was tumbling in circles, the toast and orange juice she'd consumed for breakfast threatening to return. It took everything in her to control the quiver of anxiety that was causing her hands and knees to shake.

Easing her helmet off her head, Michelle came through the gate to where they stood. She extended her hand to Greg Rockman, a warm smile filling her face. "Hey there, Uncle Greg. Glad you could make it."

"I wouldn't have missed this for anything, Mitch. You looked great out there. How did the bike handle?"

"She's sweet. We're going to have to do some work on the engine but the light weight of the body makes it a very nice ride."

"That's what I wanted to hear," the man said excitedly. "Now, you sure I can't convince you to come ride for me instead? You sure know how to handle yourself out there!"

Michelle shook her head. "I don't think so, sir. I much prefer the garage."

Michelle looked from Rockman to Mark and then noticed Vanessa eyeing her with interest. She bristled, trying to not let her sudden discomfort show.

"Oh, I'm being rude," Rockman said, moving to wrap an arm around Michelle's shoulders. "Mitch, let me introduce you to the competition. This is Mark Stall—"

Michelle cut him off. "We've met," she said curtly, the smile draining from her face.

Mark stared in awe, his mouth parted slightly as he struggled to focus. He'd not been able to mask his obvious surprise. When Michelle had taken off her helmet, pulling a hand through her hair, he'd been instantly captivated. He had barely been able to contain his excitement when he'd recognized her.

Wire mesh and steel posts had separated the asphalt from the weathered grass where he'd been standing with Rockman and Vanessa. Where Michelle had rested on the other side had felt almost miles away to Mark. Suddenly he'd wanted to jump the fenced barrier to sweep her into his arms and hold her. He shook his head slightly, waving the clouds from his thoughts. "Yes, we have. How are you, Mitch?"

Michelle's smile turned down into a deep frown. She nodded her head, not saying anything to him at all. "And how are you doing, Mrs. Stallion?" she asked, turning her attention toward Vanessa instead, loudly emphasizing the *Mrs*.

Vanessa laughed out loud. "It's Ms. Long and I'm just taking it all in," she said, unable to contain her giggles.

Michelle raised a curious eyebrow at the comment. "I'm just sure you are," she said, moving back to the motorcycle. "Well, I need to get this in the garage to see what damage has been done. If you all will excuse me."

Rockman nodded. "I'm right behind you." He shook Mark's hand a second time, giving the man a smug wink. "We'll see you in our rearview mirror, Stallion. Take it easy now."

Mark glared at the man. "You wish, Rockman. You wish." He turned his attention back to Michelle, who was now on the other side of the fence, easing her bike toward the garage bays. She wore leather. Leather jeans and a jacket that bore the Rockman Racing logo fit her petite figure nicely. Everything about her demeanor highlighted her extraordinary beauty. Her confidence and self-assurance was almost intimidating, and he found the wealth of her talent sexy as hell.

Mark winced as she pulled out of sight. It suddenly dawned on him that she was working for the competition. And worse, it appeared as if she might actually like the job. Mark couldn't begin to imagine what Michelle could possibly see in Rockman or his team. Even if he could have wooed her away with a better offer, Mark sensed that his chances of success, business or personal, didn't look favorable. That icy stare she'd given him hadn't done much at all for his self-confidence.

Vanessa's amusement had increased tenfold, and as she stood staring at Mark it was all she could do to contain her enthusiasm. The expression on the man's face was priceless. He stood staring after Michelle like a lovesick puppy, his eyes wide and sad that the exquisite woman was gone from him. Vanessa couldn't remember him ever reacting to any woman like that before. Maybe this Mitch woman had a few redeeming qualities that Vanessa didn't know about.

She grinned. "So, you just gonna stand there or do you plan on catching up with the woman to ask her out?"

"What? Huh?" Mark asked, jumping. He'd gotten lost in thought, having forgotten that Vanessa was even there. Heat warmed his dark cheeks as he blushed profusely. "What are you talking about, Vanessa?" he answered finally.

Vanessa pointed in Michelle's direction. "You need to tell her the truth and straighten your mess out. So, go do what you need to do."

Mark cringed. For the life of him he couldn't quite figure out why things seemed so complicated. It felt like that woman had gotten up under his skin and now he had a raging rash that he couldn't quite scratch. He shook his head, trying to shake every thought of Michelle out of his head. He shrugged his broad shoulders. "Leave it alone," he said, his tone short as a bold-faced lie passed over his lips. "She's not interested and neither am I."

Michelle rarely ran into other women in the ladies' room of the racetrack when the tracks were closed to the public, so running into Vanessa Long took her completely by surprise. Each and every time she'd thought that perhaps she could have been wrong about Mark Stallion, his so-called fiancée had been by his side and Michelle had changed her mind. Obviously the two were closer than he'd wanted her to know or he wouldn't have lied about them being together. If Michelle was certain of anything, she knew that she didn't need that kind of drama in her life, so Michelle had made avoiding him and his woman a scientific art. And now, with her bladder about to burst, she truly had no interest in dealing with Vanessa soon-to-be-married Long.

As she'd made her way into the five-stall space, pulling at the zipper to her jeans, she had no interest in dealing with Vanessa, who stood at the oversize mirror freshening her makeup. The other woman broke out into a full grin at the sight of her.

"Hey, what's up?" Vanessa called out, addressing her as if they were longtime friends.

Michelle's eyebrows were raised curiously as she nodded her greeting, caught too off guard to speak.

Vanessa turned an about-face as Michelle rushed into the closest stall and closed the door. Behind her, Vanessa laughed out loud.

"What's so funny?" Michelle asked, her voice carrying through the door.

"You. You had to know that we'd run into each other sooner or later."

"Actually, I hadn't given it much thought," Michelle answered.

"I'm sure you wished it wouldn't happen at all is what I'm sure you were thinking."

Michelle flushed the commode, then made her way back out to the row of sinks that lined the wall. She tossed Vanessa a quick glance as she turned on the faucet, reached for the liquid soap and washed her hands. "You give yourself too much credit," she said. "Truly, I haven't given you much thought at all," she said.

Vanessa laughed again. "But I'm sure my friend Mark's been on your mind. I'm sure he's been on your mind a lot."

Vanessa calling the man's name made Michelle bristle ever so slightly. Despite her best efforts, emotion showed on her face, her interest and frustration with the man gleaming out of her eyes.

Vanessa nodded anxiously. "Looks like I got that one right," she said smugly.

Michelle reached for a paper towel. "Look, I don't have any issues with you. In fact, I'm very happy for you and Mr. Stallion. I'm sure you two will make a lovely couple."

"I don't think so," Vanessa said, crossing her arms over her chest as she leaned back against the bathroom wall. "Mark's not my type."

For the first time since entering the room, Michelle turned to stare directly at the woman. "Excuse me?"

"My type. He's not my type."

"They why are you marrying him?"

"I'm not. Not really. It's just a little joke I play on him every now and then."

"And he finds your joke funny?"

"Usually. But this time he wasn't laughing with me." Vanessa shook her head, humor still washing over her expression. "Go figure," she said, crossing her arms.

Michelle shook her head. "Whatever. It sounds to me like you and your friend enjoy playing your games."

"He's been known to play and win a few. Mark likes taking risks."

"Well, I don't have time for his games or him," Michelle said emphatically.

Vanessa shrugged. "You're a little uptight, aren't you? Mark usually isn't attracted to uptight women. I'm surprised."

Michelle's annoyance was acute as she shifted her weight to her left hip, both of her hands at her waist. "Where do you get off thinking you can—" Michelle started.

Vanessa interrupted her, stopping her in her tracks. "Oh, don't get your nipples twisted. I was just teasing. Look, Mark really likes you. You should give him another chance. He really is a great guy."

Michelle turned back to stare at her. "Why do you care?"

"He's my friend. My *best* friend. And like I said, he likes you. He likes you a lot and I've never known him to be interested in any woman like he seems to be interested in you. So that means there's something special about you and my best friend deserves special."

Vanessa moved to stand in front of Michelle, extending her hand in greeting. "Let's start over again. I'm Vanessa, a friend of the Stallion family. It's nice to meet you, Mitch."

Michelle found herself extending her own hand as Vanessa shook it warmly. "It's nice to meet you, too," she said, reservation still tinting her words.

"So, my boy's been trying real hard to get your attention and you've been giving him one heck of a time. What does a brother need to do?"

Michelle shrugged. "I don't know. I guess I need to think about it more."

"Well, don't think too hard. All that thinking isn't good for you. Just go for it. I promise you he really is an incredible guy. Any woman would be lucky to have him."

"So why aren't you interested?" Michelle asked curiously.

Vanessa's gaze swept from the top of Michelle's head down to the tips of her steel-toed boots. She stepped in closer, the scent of her body spray filling the space between them. Winking, Vanessa brushed the back of her fingers down the length of Michelle's arm. "Like I said, he's not my type," she said, her voice coming in a husky whisper.

Understanding rained down over Michelle as Vanessa raised her eyes suggestively. She took a quick step back, discomfort puddling around her spirit. "Oh," she said quickly. "Oh."

Vanessa laughed again. "Girlfriend, you look like you've seen a ghost! I'm not that scary," she said warmly. "And, I promise not to bite. Unless of course you want me to?" she said, her eyebrows pushing skyward a second time.

Michelle laughed nervously. "No, thanks. I'll pass."

"Good. I'd hate to break Mark's heart again. He hates it when I get the pretty girls and he doesn't."

Amusement crossed Michelle's face. "I'm sure he does."

Vanessa tossed her another wink. "Hey, I've got a question for you," she said, switching subjects just like that. "Everyone says you're the resident bike wizard around here. What's the maximum weight for a Pro Stock bike?"

Michelle chuckled, her arms folding over her chest. "It depends on the engine combination. What are you riding?"

"Nothing but a Harley, baby!"

"Six hundred and fifteen pounds and that includes the rider. Are you thinking about racing?"

"No, I just wanted to know if what they said about you was true."

This time Michelle snickered. "Did I pass the test?"

Vanessa grinned. "I like you, Mitch. I think you and I will be good friends."

Vanessa moved past Michelle, pulling at the handle on the door. She tossed a quick glance over her shoulder. "Please," she intoned, the gesture just shy of being a whine, "give my boy some play. He's starting to be a real pain in my left cheek," she said, as she gave Michelle a quick wave of her hand.

Nodding, Michelle laughed with her. "We'll see what happens," she answered, following Vanessa.

Vanessa smiled. "And if it doesn't work out…" she started.

Michelle shook her head. "No thanks, Vanessa. I don't roll like that."

Vanessa shrugged, sighing deeply. "Well, you can't blame a girl for trying!"

Michelle had kicked the tire of Simon's old pickup truck. Of all times for the battery to die on her, it had to happen when she most wanted to make a quick getaway. To add insult to injury, there wasn't a tool to be found inside the truck or out. She surely planned to send her uncle to his afterlife the minute she saw him. She was ready to kill the old geezer for putting her in such a predicament.

Her standing in the middle of a convenience store parking lot with a motorcycle strapped securely in the bed of the truck, wearing heels and a short skirt was hardly going unnoticed. For Mark Stallion to be pulling into the parking lot while she'd been trying to pull out couldn't have made for worse timing.

She'd taken extra effort not to run into him at the racetrack. A few of her father's old friends had been keeping an eye out for her, keeping her abreast of his comings and goings. Only occasionally had she stopped to watch him go through his paces, taking his turn around the course to prepare for the upcoming time trials. After her conversation with Vanessa she'd made more of an effort to keep her eye on him, to determine if she needed to reconsider her position, but she wasn't ready for any close and personal encounters with him just yet.

Watching him so often though had her wondering if maybe she should give the man half a chance, but Michelle wasn't keen on giving any man another opportunity to hurt her heart. One man too many had stomped her emotions big time and she'd learned early that she wasn't a woman who was a glutton for punishment.

Today, nothing had gone right for Michelle. The day had started badly and seemed to be getting worse with each passing minute. She'd purposely left the tracks early, not wanting to risk seeing that man or any other, and now, here she was, hiding out like she'd been the one to do something wrong. She had ducked down into her seat the minute she'd seen him step from his black sedan, moving into the store to pay for gasoline at the pumps. She'd been certain he'd not seen her and Michelle was determined to keep it that way. Peeking up at her rearview mirror, she tried to see if he was still inside or not. Rising slightly, she turned to peer over her right shoulder, looking to see if he was moving about inside. She was hardly prepared for the loud knock that came from her left, the tapping heavy against the driver's window.

Mark was smiling sheepishly as he rapped quickly on the glass window, leaning to peer inside. "Hey, the clerk said it looked like you were having some trouble. Is everything okay?" he questioned curiously, amused at the look that blessed her face. Clearly, Michelle was not thrilled to see him.

Michelle took a deep breath, holding it for a brief moment before she opened the car door and stepped outside. Mark stepped back just enough to give her room, still standing close enough for the light scent of his cologne to tease her senses. Michelle felt a quiver of energy flood through her body, traveling the length of her spine. She clutched her fists tight against her body, trying to stall the rise of wanting that seemed to surface with a vengeance.

"I'm just fine, thank you."

"He said it looked like your truck wouldn't start."

"He didn't know what he was talking about," Michelle said, fighting not to stare into his eyes.

Mark nodded slowly. "Well, if you do need help…"

"I don't," Michelle said cutting him off.

"Mitch, look…"

"No, you look. Why are you bothering me? Can't you take the hint?"

Mark bit down against his tongue. Clearly she wasn't going to make this easy on him. "I need to explain about Vanessa. She and I really aren't engaged."

Thoughts of her conversation with Vanessa crossed Michelle's mind and she tried not to let her amusement at Mark's discomfort show on her face. "That's your problem," she said nonchalantly. "It's not mine."

Mark continued, pushing past the wall that Michelle was trying to build between them. "It was a joke. Kind of like a game she and I—"

Michelle interrupted him. "I don't particularly care for you or your games, Mr. Stallion, so if you'll excuse me."

Mark shook his head, still staring at her. Her stubbornness intrigued him. He'd noticed her kicking her car tire, obviously frustrated by something. The college student manning the registers inside had been watching her intently as well, the young man's comments causing Mark to prickle with a hint of jealousy. He didn't want any other man admiring Michelle like that. But even he couldn't deny that she would certainly pique a man's interest. She had *his* full attention.

Eyeing her up and down, he took in her long legs, the sculpted limbs appearing even longer beneath the short wisp of skirt she wore. As if Michelle was reading his mind, she gave the hemline a quick tug, color flooding her full cheeks. She took a quick breath of fresh air and the lush curve of her breasts rose up and then down as she blew the warm breath back out. Her gaze was lowered, avoiding his, and Mark couldn't help but be amused at her stubbornness. She met his stare and looked away quickly, her discomfort more than obvious.

Her mouth parted ever so slightly as she pushed the tip of her tongue out to moisten her lips. The motion was slow and deliberate and as he watched her a rush of heat rained into Mark's southern quadrant. He felt himself break out into a cold sweat. Before he realized what he was doing, Mark took a step forward, gliding his right arm around her waist. The gesture caught Michelle completely off guard and before she could comprehend what was happening, Mark kissed her, his full lips gliding like silk against her own.

Chapter 7

Although the left side of his face still stung from the slap Michelle had given him, Mark was all grins. As he made his way home he couldn't stop thinking about the kiss the two of them had just shared. That kiss had been well worth the resounding slam her right palm had given his cheek because for just a brief moment Michelle had kissed him back, working her lips nicely against his own.

She'd gently suckled his bottom lip, a hint of tongue caressing his upper lip and just as he'd clutched her body tighter to his, Michelle had stiffened, pushing him from her. Then she'd slapped him. That kiss had been the sweetest connection he had ever had with any woman. Michelle had tasted like strawberries. Ripe, sweet fruit that had him wishing for more. The only thing Mark regretted was not being able to wind back time and do it all over again.

After tossing her a quick wink, his palm rubbing the bruise

across his face, he'd left her standing there, staring after him as he'd moved back to his own car. Neither had uttered a word, having no clue what they should say. Mark shook his head. Usually he was a lot smoother than that but something about Michelle Coleman had all his smooth ruffled to high hell.

Mark shuddered. Every muscle in his body had gone hard with desire. The last remnant of a full erection was still pulling taut in his briefs. His head was still foggy. He was dismayed at how his body had flagrantly given his heart away. He had wanted her. Badly. Pretending otherwise would only have been a lie. Chuckling softly, Mark could only imagine what Michelle had to have been thinking right about then.

All Michelle could think of was a cold shower. She desperately needed one quick. She needed one to stall the rise of heat that had consumed every square inch of her flesh. She still couldn't believe that he had kissed her like that and the fact that she had kissed him back was wrecking total havoc on her nerves. She had kissed him back and had enjoyed every second of it and now she was burning hot from the inside out, feeling as if she was about to combust from the longing. The minute his lips had touched hers the experience had become surreal. The man had the mouth of a god and Michelle had felt blessed beyond measure.

She pressed two fingers to her lips, the flesh still tingling with pleasure. Every spot where his body had touched hers was still throbbing, her senses heightened like never before. She could still taste him, the flavor like decadent chocolate against her tongue. She could still smell him, the scent so intense she felt as if it was seeping from her own pores. To add insult to injury she was so hungry for him that Michelle knew if he were still standing before her she would have opened herself gladly, beckoning him inside as if her life depended on it. She felt like she was about to explode. She needed a cold shower, quick, and the time it was taking AAA to jump-start her engine felt like forever.

Greg Rockman had pulled his car off to the side of the road as he caught sight of his star mechanic in a tight embrace with his nemesis. The two had been standing in the parking lot of the Motorplex Convenience Station clutching each other with quiet abandon.

It had just crossed Rockman's mind to question why Michelle was kissing Stallion when the woman had slapped the man. Hard. So hard that it had swung Stallion's head over to the side, rattling his teeth. Rockman knew that slap had hurt because it had hurt him to see it. He touched his own jaw in sympathy.

Rockman could feel the muscles in his face pull his mouth into a wide smile. That slap had made his day. Bringing down Mark Stallion was going to be easier than he'd imagined and he surely wanted to knock the Stallions down a peg or two.

Pulling back into traffic, Rockman was amused that Michelle would play into his plans so easily. Her presence around the race circuit had become an annoyance, too many people willing to answer too many questions about that father of hers. All those stories had her asking questions that she didn't need any answers to.

The man swiped a palm across his brow, and then pulled at the length of necktie around his thick neck. His day had been long and from the looks of things that wasn't going to change anytime soon. He'd been spending an exorbitant amount of time running interference between Michelle and folks who had way too much information to share. Reminding other people that silence was truly the best policy took some quiet maneuvering. He didn't need Michelle asking the wrong person the right question, because having an answer that pointed too close to him was not a good thing. Rockman was a man with many secrets and he preferred to keep it that way.

Hiring Michelle had given him some leverage. Her skills would not only be useful to his organization, but she'd be close enough for him to keep an eye on. If things continued the way they were going, Rockman thought, then he might have to change his tactics and that wouldn't be good. He didn't want to see things end badly for Michelle, he mused as he headed for downtown Dallas. Truth be told, he really did like the girl.

It was well after midnight when Michelle's telephone rang. The young woman was still wide awake, unable to drift off to sleep. She couldn't stop thinking about her day, and that man, and then her phone rang. Reaching for the receiver, she didn't bother to look at the caller ID, never imagining that Mark Stallion would be calling her after she had slapped his face. She was surprised to hear his voice on the other end.

"Hey, Mitch, I didn't wake you, did I?"

Michelle paused, transfixed by the liquid silk of his deep baritone voice as it seeped over the phone line. The sound of his voice reawakened every emotion her two cold showers had washed away.

"Mitch? You still there?" Mark asked, hoping that she'd not hung up on him.

"Yes. And no, you didn't wake me."

Mark smiled into the receiver. "I'm sorry to call so late, but…" He paused, not having an excuse why he'd chosen this time over any other. All he knew was that he hadn't been able to sleep. Michelle hadn't left his thoughts since that afternoon, and their kiss, and so he'd called, hoping against all odds that she would speak with him. When she'd actually picked up the call he'd been ecstatic. The fact that she was still on the other end, speaking with him, was pure butter cream icing on some very sweet cake.

"I just wanted to hear your voice," he said, his own trailing off quietly.

Michelle didn't say anything at all, a quiver of something she couldn't quite name erupting from her core. She was on fire again and she wanted to be bothered by it but couldn't find any reason to be annoyed.

"Why?" she finally questioned.

Mark took a deep breath, then answered. "I felt like you and I had made a nice connection the other week at my sister-in-law's party. If you'll give me a chance, I really want to see where you and I might be able to take that."

"And, what about your girlfriend?"

Mark smiled. "Vanessa's my friend. Not my *girlfriend*. She's a lesbian. I'm definitely not her type."

Michelle raised a teasing eyebrow. "Sure she is. You think I'll fall for anything, don't you?"

"Not at all. It's the truth. Vanessa is gay. She doesn't like men and she surely doesn't like me. Not like that."

"So why does she go around telling people you two are engaged, or married, or whatever lie it is that you two tell?"

Mark took a deep breath before answering. "It's a bad habit we used to have. If either of us was in a situation that we needed to get out of, the other would come to the rescue."

"And she needed to rescue you from me that night?"

"No, not at all. She just didn't know it, is all."

"Uh-huh."

"Really, Mitch. In the past I wasn't looking for any permanent relationship. If it looked like a woman wanted more than I was interested in giving, Vanessa would just kind of head them off at the pass."

"And you've suddenly changed your ways?"

"I just know that I'd like an opportunity to get to know you better and I want you to get to know the real me."

Pondering what he'd said, Michelle didn't respond. Mark listened to her breathing quietly on the other end. The silence was awkward, but he would have taken awkward, uncomfortable and anything else if it moved the two of them closer.

"You really pack a mean right hook," Mark finally said, breaking the silence.

Michelle giggled. "I didn't hit you with a right hook. If I had I doubt you'd be able to speak at all right now."

"Remind me never to make you mad again."

"I wasn't mad."

"Then why did you hit me?"

"Reflex. I don't take kindly to men putting their hands on me without an invitation."

"The way you were looking at me I thought I'd been invited."

"Well, you thought wrong."

Mark chuckled. "Sorry about that but I just couldn't resist."

"Try harder next time."

"Are you going to give me a next time?"

"Good night, Mr. Stallion."

"Mark."

"Good night, Mark."

"Don't hang up," Mark called out anxiously, lifting himself up off the pillows he'd been resting on. "Have dinner with me tonight. Please, Mitch?"

Michelle held the receiver away from her, her eyes pressed tightly shut. She so wanted to say yes that the word was on the tip of her tongue, eager and anxious to fall out of her mouth. But instead, she hung up the telephone, disconnecting the call. After replacing the receiver on the hook, Michelle pulled her knees to her chest, curling her body in a fetal position against the mattress. She didn't have a clue why she wasn't willing to give the man a chance, but trusting Mark Stallion with his less-than-stellar reputation didn't feel like a very smart thing for her to do.

Over the years, she'd been around enough men to know that most were usually up to no good. It had been common practice for the boys to brag about their conquests and relationship successes and failures. Her father had been very protective of her and had made her promise time and time again to not allow any man to take advantage of her. The few relationships Michelle had ventured to establish had all ended badly, causing her much heartache. Shortly after her father's death, Michelle's attitude toward most men in general had gone hard. It had taken much conviction and fortitude to develop the thick skin she now wore like a badge of honor to cover the relationship wounds that had messed with her head. But she really liked Mark Stallion. She was curious to know him better, but after what was clearly a rocky start she wasn't sure she was ready or willing to let down her guard.

On the other side of town Mark was still holding his own cell phone to his chest. The conversation had gone far better than he'd anticipated. She hadn't slammed the telephone down when she'd first heard his voice, allowing him to at least kick off a conversation between them. That had to count for something. He leaned back against the mound of pillows that cradled his head, blowing a deep sigh of relief. Things between him and Michelle were starting to look up, he thought.

Hearing her voice had ignited a spark of something inside him that he couldn't quite recognize. The deep alto tone had been bewitching, teasing his senses, and all he could think of was kissing her again, and again. He'd gotten happy the minute she'd spoken his name. Happy like he'd never been happy before. The emotion had been as basic as any he'd ever experienced before and now he was swimming in the wealth of it. The sensation was warm and comforting and Mark was thoroughly enjoying how that felt.

He was surprised when the device in his hand rang, the familiar ringtone chiming loudly. Pulling it to his ear, he flipped the unit open and said hello, curiosity seeping from his voice.

Michelle responded from the other end. "Are you free tomorrow afternoon at about four o'clock?" she asked, just a hint of nervousness painting her words.

Mark nodded into the receiver, oblivious to the fact that she couldn't see him. "If it means I can spend time with you, I'll make myself free."

Michelle smiled. "Meet me at the Redline Raceway."

"Redline? In Caddo Mills?"

"Yes, take Interstate 30 east. The track is about twenty miles outside of Dallas. You're about twenty minutes away when you cross over Lake Hubbard."

"I'll be there," Mark said, excitement brimming in his voice. "Four o'clock! Should I bring anything?"

"Yes, your bike. Have a good night, Mark."

"Good night, Mitch," he said before he disconnected his end of the call. He grinned. Things were definitely starting to look up.

Chapter 8

A meeting of the Stallion Enterprises executive board had been called to order. The four Stallion brothers sat around the large conference table reviewing the multitude of documents that littered the top. They'd been at it for over four hours when Mark flipped his ballpoint pen out of his hand and onto a manila folder he'd just slammed shut. The abrasive gesture was a major distraction, causing them all to stop what they'd been doing.

"What's the matter with you?" John asked, eyeing Mark curiously.

Mark shrugged broad shoulders. "Man, it's seventy-eight degrees and sunny outside and I'm stuck here inside with you three. What could possibly be wrong with that?" he said facetiously.

John rolled his dark eyes then cast a look toward Matthew. "Would you please remind your brother that being a part of

this organization's senior staff comes with some responsibilities, the least of which is the devotion of his time to executive matters."

Matthew chuckled. "You remind him. I'd rather be out there
right now, too," he answered, slapping a high five with Mark.

"He's just not focused this morning," Luke interjected.
"He's got a date later today."

"A date? With who, I wonder?" John said, looking smugly
from one brother to the other.

"And just where did you hear that?" Mark questioned,
shifting anxiously in his seat. "I never said I had a date."

Luke laughed. "No, you didn't, did you? I wonder why?"
The young man paused before continuing. "Yeah, why didn't
you want us to know you're going out with my friend Mitch
tonight, Mark?"

"What's up with that?" Matthew added. "Does this
Mitch have an extra eye or two heads that you're embarrassed about?"

The brothers all laughed.

John shook his head. "No, bro. Mitch is fine. But I think
she could take Mark in a wrestling match."

"What do you mean?" Mark asked, an incredulous expression washing over his face.

Matthew laughed. "She must be built like a linebacker. Is
that it, John?"

The oldest sibling chuckled. "Nah, guy, I'm telling you
Mitch is one gorgeous woman but she's tough as nails. Baby
girl doesn't play. She would hurt Mark."

"I don't believe you just said that," Mark said, flipping a
hand in his brother's direction.

Luke interjected. "John's got a point. Besides, she's got you
soft, big brother! Mitch has got you soft like Play-Doh."

His three brothers burst out laughing and Mark couldn't help but laugh with them.

"It's not like that," he said, finally composing himself. "It's just…well…she…" he stammered, searching for the right words to try to explain to his three best friends what he was feeling for Michelle.

Matthew threw his hands up. "I swear! Not you, too!" he exclaimed loudly.

"What?"

"You're acting just like John did when he fell in love with Marah."

"How'd I act?" John asked, an air of defensiveness rising in his tone. "I didn't act any different from how I usually act."

"Oh, yes you did," Luke said with a smile. "You got all soft and gushy anytime someone mentioned your wife's name."

"I did not!"

"Yes, you did," Matthew said, agreeing with his sibling. "Even Mark knows you did. Don't you, bro?" Matthew didn't wait for the man to answer. "Now, I think the love bug done bit Mark on the behind, too."

Mark's eyes rolled toward the coffered ceiling as he flipped his hand at his brother, dismissing him. Rising from his seat, he strolled over to the window and looked out over the Dallas skyline. "You don't know what you're talking about," he said finally, purposely ignoring the three sets of eyes watching him closely.

John laughed. "Well, I'm going to hate to see you when you do get to know her 'cause you've got it bad."

"Real bad," Luke said.

"Real, real bad," Matthew added.

Mark continued to stare out over the city, not bothering to respond. He hated it when he knew his brothers were right.

* * *

Mark could smell engine fuel and burning tires the minute he stepped out of his car. He breathed deeply, filling his lungs with the dank aromas. He had trailered one of his race bikes behind his Lincoln Navigator, not quite sure what Michelle had in store for him. His heart skipped a beat, and then two, as Michelle caught sight of him searching her out. As she moved in his direction he could feel himself grinning foolishly. Michelle was smiling as widely when she maneuvered over to his side.

She extended a hand toward him, welcoming him politely. "I'm glad you could join us, Mark."

Mark raised an eyebrow at the "us" comment. He wasn't quite sure who "us" was and he'd been hoping for some one-on-one time with Michelle. He hadn't been prepared for any group activity. He looked around anxiously. "Thank you for inviting me. So, what's going on here?" he asked curiously.

Michelle gestured with her head toward the blacktopped course that made up the raceway. "A few of us come out here to do some drag racing every now and then. I thought I could just see what you're made of," Michelle said casually. She tossed him a wide smile of brilliant pearl-white teeth.

Mark suddenly felt like he would melt right where he stood. The temperature around them had risen with a vengeance and he was feeling very heated. He pushed his hands deep into the pockets of his denim jeans, trying to stall the wave of nervous energy that had passed through him. The front of his pants suddenly pinched a little too tight for comfort.

"You do know how to run a drag?" Michelle asked teasingly. "It doesn't scare you, does it?"

Mark laughed. "You're funny, Mitch. I like that. A woman with jokes!"

Michelle shrugged. "You turned a little green—that's why I was asking," she said, noting his discomfort.

Mark nodded. "Okay, green! I hear you."

Michelle gestured with her hand for him to follow along behind her. "Get your bike and come on," she said as she headed in the direction of the service pits. "Let me introduce you."

Eleven race bikes were lined in a neat row. A crowd of bike enthusiasts and drivers were crowded around in conversation, loud laughter ringing through the afternoon air. Michelle signaled with her index finger for him to join her. After some quick introductions, one of the bike group organizers laid down the rules. The man who everyone called Dust was tall, taller than Mark, with a wide forehead and blistering blue-green eyes.

"Okay, we're going to run a few heats. You all know how this goes. It's two-vehicle, tournament-style eliminations. We're running a quarter-mile track. Fastest acceleration to the finish line wins. The losing driver in each race is eliminated and the winning driver will progress until the last man, or woman—" he nodded at Michelle and three other females by her side "—is standing. Any questions?"

A young man who barely looked old enough to race pushed up his hand. "Yeah," he said gruffly, "who's holding the cash?"

The others shook their heads as Dust answered, "Keep the cash in your pocket, Tyler. We'll ante up after the race."

"Well, I don't trust some of you!" Tyler exclaimed. "Just make sure you all don't run off with my money when I whip you."

Michelle laughed. "Give it up, Tyler. You know one of us is going to wear you out in the first round. Just don't cry when we do."

Tyler scowled, grunting his response. Mark grinned,

thinking the afternoon was going to be better than he thought. He eased up to Michelle's side.

"So, what are the bets?"

"It's a minimum of five hundred dollars for each run. Loser pays the winner. All side bets are gravy."

"Is there a maximum?"

Michelle cut her eye up at him. "Well, I guess that depends."

"On what?"

"On just how good you think you are."

Mark chuckled. "No, that depends on how good you are. I was going to bet all my money on you, babe."

Michelle blushed, color flooding her face as he shook her head. "You've got the second leg," she said finally. "You're racing Tyler. Don't embarrass yourself, because he can't ride worth beans. If he beats you, you will never live it down."

Smiling, he nodded. "I promise not to disappoint you," he said, tossing her a quick wink.

And he didn't. By the fifth race, Mark was going toe-to-toe with Michelle. He sat revving his engine, grinning as she eased her bike up to the starting line. She lifted the visor to her helmet and gave him a smile that had his heart beating like a steel drum in his chest.

"Let's you and I sweeten the pot a bit," Mark ventured, his eyes widening with excitement.

Michelle eyed him with reservation. "What do you have in mind?"

Mark grinned. "Just a side bet between the two of us. If I win you'll buy me dinner this weekend. And I'm easy to please. A good steak and baked potato will suit me just fine."

For a brief moment Michelle studied him, his hopeful expression causing a ripple of warmth through her abdomen. She gave him a coy smile then nodded. "I can do that," she said, her voice feeling like silk against his ears. "But," she added, causing Mark to stiffen momentarily with anxiety. "If I win you'll buy me dinner *and* breakfast the next morning." She lifted her eyebrows suggestively.

There was a pregnant pause as Mark took in her comment, allowing it to mull over in his mind, comprehension coming slowly. He suddenly laughed at her brazenness, the woman surprising the heck out of him. It was a loud, deep laugh that caused everyone to turn and stare to see what was so funny. Dropping her visor back down, Michelle revved her own engine then gave him a quick thumbs-up sign. Before Mark knew what had happened, Michelle was eyeing him out of her side mirror, her dust kissing him sweetly. As he rolled into second place, thoughts of what might lie ahead for the two of them made losing better than any win he could have imagined.

From his favorite seat in the bleachers Greg Rockman sat watching one of his competitors take laps around the track. Jack Crenshaw, a rival team owner sat three rows in front of him. He was a burly man with a ruddy complexion known most for the apple-scented tobacco he smoked out of an intricately carved pipe. Like most of the other owners, he had no use for Rockman.

"Your guy looks a little shaky going around the turns, Jack. Did he pass that drug test?"Rockman asked with an annoying chortle.

"You know, Rockman, if you spent more time worrying about your own drivers and not mine, some of them might actually last a season with you. Just how many of your guys bailed out of their contracts last year? I heard you lost a few good men."

"Well, you heard wrong. Besides, if they're gone from my payroll, then they weren't too good to start off with,"

Rockman chuckled. "I've got a solid team, Jack, and we're going to own all of you boys before it's all said and done."

Jack laughed. "So, tell me, how'd you manage to snare Mitch Coleman? I've got to give you your props for that catch."

"When you got it, you got it. What can I say?"

"Uh-huh," Jack muttered, cringing with distaste. He was grateful Rockman couldn't see his face as he still sat with his back to the man. His dislike for the man dripped from his pores, Rockman grating on his nerves like an annoying bug. "Well," he said, his gaze still following the driver out on the course, "when you screw that up there's a long line of us ready to truly appreciate her skills. Personally, if I were a betting man I'd put my money on Mitch lasting two weeks before she sees you for the pond scum that you are. She'll be headed for higher ground right after."

Rockman bristled ever so slightly, a smile still plastered across his round face. "Just goes to show what you don't know, Jack. Mitch is as loyal as they come."

"So was her father and we know where that got him, don't we now?" John asked, turning about in his seat to meet the other man's gaze.

Rockman's stare was pure ice, boring a hole straight through Jack's heart. He shifted forward in his seat, slowly stroking the length of beard that covered his chin. When he spoke, his tone was low, the intonation ringing with hostility. "I don't know what you're trying to imply, but Brent Coleman's death was a horrible tragedy. You soil his memory to speak ill of him like that. Now, he was a very good friend and I loved him dearly. I'm also glad that I can be here for his daughter now." He sat back, still eyeing Jack with venom.

The other man shrugged. "Rockman, with you for a friend I'm sure Brent didn't need any enemies. Besides, I don't think

Brent's daughter is as gullible as you would like her to be. Seems she's been asking a lot of questions about her father's *accident*. Questions the rest of us would like some answers to as well."

Before Rockman could voice a response, they heard the loud skid of burning tires and the horrific crash that resounded through the air. Both turned just in time to see the bike, minus its rider, explode across the track. Jack jumped from his seat, moving to get out of the bleachers and down below as quickly as he could.

Behind him Rockman stood staring, his expression blank as he watched the hustle of activity rushing below. The faint bend of his lips pulled at his facial muscles as he fought the desire to grin widely. He pulled at the lapels of his jacket, adjusting the lightweight coat around his large frame.

The man heaved a deep sigh. So, Michelle was still asking questions about her father. He had hoped her need to know more would have died down after the investigation had ruled the crash an accident, but it looked like having her back at the tracks had only served to further fuel her curiosity.

After Brent's death, Rockman had worked hard to insure that Michelle trusted him. He'd been there to support her, helping with the funeral expenses and eventually investing in the young woman's garage venture. He'd known that Michelle was talented, her skills superior to most, and he'd given her more than enough time to get past her grief before offering her a job that would bring them closer together.

Rockman's interest in Michelle went above and beyond a paternal concern. His need to keep Michelle under his wing and close to his heart had become a quiet obsession. He regretted that his friend Brent had discovered his predilection for the girl, everything about Michelle reminding him of her mother.

Rockman had never loved any woman the way he'd loved Olivia Coleman. He'd loved Olivia well before she'd met and married his buddy Brent. He'd been a third wheel with the duo, both considering him nothing more than an old friend. Watching the woman he adored loving his best buddy had made him resentful. The day the woman had walked away from her family had been bittersweet. Olivia had left Brent, but nothing Rockman had said or done had convinced her to walk into his arms instead.

Rockman had feigned being friends with Brent, hoping against all odds that he could run interference on any reconciliation between the couple, but Olivia had never returned, leaving all of them behind. The one perk had been Michelle, the pigtailed tomboy whose engaging smile and spirited personality had epitomized everything Rockman had loved about her mother. Then his infatuation with the child had become less than stellar.

Rockman remembered well the moment Michelle's father had caught him in the family home, Michelle perched innocently on his knee. There had been something about how he'd been looking at the child that had raised a red flag with her father. The man's questions and then resounding demand that Rockman stay away from them both hadn't been well received. Rockman had become embittered and resentful and an all-out war had been waged between them.

Brent's resignation and threats to expose him just hours before that fatal race had been the final straw, the two men swearing themselves bitter enemies. Keeping everyone else from finding out, had been everything and Rockman had played every card he had to win that hand permanently. Severing Brent's brake line had been easy. Years of hatred for the man had made Rockman indifferent to the consequences.

Rockman continued to stare down at the activity below as track personnel worked to contain the gathering crowd and an EMS crew administered to the fallen man. Too bad about Jack's driver, Rockman thought to himself. It was surely too bad that crap had to happen to good people.

Chapter 9

Michelle stood in the shower allowing the spray of warm water to wash down over her face. She still couldn't believe she'd said what she'd said. *Dinner and breakfast!* As if that left anything to the imagination. The moment and the comment had been haunting her for days. Not only did that man have her feeling foolish but here she was acting foolish as well. She couldn't begin to explain what had come over her. It was as if the heat had gotten right to her brain and had fried all her good judgment.

She leaned against the shower wall trying to figure out how she was going to get out of the mess she'd gotten herself into. She surely needed to halt any thoughts Mark Stallion might have about the two of them spending the night together. A quiver of heat rushed through her feminine spirit. Thinking about spending the night with Mark suddenly had her breathing heavy, her body temperature rising warmer than the water that washed over her. She groaned, loudly, the sound echoing around the small room. What in the world had she gotten herself into?

An hour later when her doorbell rang, Michelle was tempted not to answer. It briefly crossed her mind to leave Mark standing on the other side until he grew weary of waiting and turned back around for his own home. But she didn't, pulling the door open anxiously to greet him.

"Please, come on in," she said softly, eyeing him from head to toe. Mark was dressed in cotton, a casual tan suit and white shirt adorning his dark complexion nicely. Michelle couldn't help but think that he was a walking billboard for *GQ* magazine, looking like he could easily grace the cover with his smoldering good looks and stylish silhouette.

"Thank you," Mark answered as he stepped inside the doorway. He was suddenly at a loss for words, his stare frozen on the beauty before him. Michelle looked radiant in a teal-green, halter-style dress that fit her curves nicely. Long legs and sandaled feet peeked from a ruffled hemline and her full bustline hinted at there being more than a mouthful for a man to handle. She was beautiful and he told her so.

"You look stunning," he said, appreciation seeping from his eyes.

Michelle blushed, color tingeing her face a vibrant red. Michelle was used to men looking at her blatantly, but Mark's admiration felt very different from the crude advances she usually got from guys. Michelle realized she liked how this felt. She liked it a lot. "Thank you," she said softly, stepping aside so that he could ease past her. "Would you like to sit down?"

Taking in his surroundings, Mark was impressed. The home was spotless, the decor simple and elegant, not at all what he'd been expecting. Michelle clearly had a flair for interior design, the elements nicely put together. Everything about the space defied what he thought he knew about her and Mark realized he didn't really know her at all. He was suddenly excited at the prospect of discovering everything he could about the woman.

"I'm glad we're doing this," he said, taking a seat against an ice-blue chenille sofa. "I'm really excited that we're going to actually spend some time together."

Michelle nodded. "So am I."

He looked around the living space a second time, taking in the Asian art on the walls, a bronze sculpture that decorated the corner of the living room, and the warm mahogany furniture that warmed the space. "You have a beautiful home. I'm surprised," he said, the compliment suddenly coming out wrong. "I mean I wasn't expecting it to look so nice. I mean…" He shook his head.

Michelle laughed. "I think I know what you mean. You figured a grease monkey like me wouldn't know a china cabinet from a china pattern, is that it?"

Mark shrugged. "Well, I guess I made some bad assumptions."

"Not bad necessarily, just wrong. I know my way around a lot more than just an engine."

The man nodded. "That's certainly obvious. And you clean up nicely as well."

Michelle giggled again. "What, you don't like my coveralls?"

"Not nearly as much as I like you in a dress," he answered with a broad smile. "Woman, you can definitely wear a dress."

Michelle rolled her eyes. She quickly changed the subject. "So, can I get you anything? Something to drink?"

Mark shook his head. "Actually, we really should be going, it's almost ten o'clock and our first reservation is for three o'clock this afternoon," he said as he came to his feet.

Michelle reached for her purse and silk wrap off the hall entry table. "So, where are we going that we need to be there so early, Mr. Stallion?"

Pressing his hand against her elbow as he guided her out the door, Mark gave a smug smile. "It's a surprise."

"I don't like surprises."

Mark laughed. "For some reason I knew that about you but I think you'll like this one. Besides, where we're having dinner isn't what's important. Where we're having breakfast is far more exciting," he said smugly. "Did you pack an overnight bag?"

"Breakfast? Overnight bag?" Michelle suddenly found herself stammering, English feeling like a foreign language she couldn't speak or comprehend.

"Oh, don't breakfast me like you don't know what I'm talking about. You won your bet fair and square and I've never been a man to renege on a bet." Mark winked suggestively as he continued. "Don't worry about the overnight bag. I've taken care of everything."

Michelle shook her head as they made their way to his car. "I'm sure I'm not going to like this at all," she said out loud, curiosity coursing through her thoughts.

The warmth of Mark's laughter filled the afternoon air as he opened the passenger side door for her. "I guess we'll just have to see," he said, chuckling. "We'll just have to see."

Chapter 10

Michelle stared out the window of Stallion Enterprises' private jet. It was as if they were floating on the clouds, the gossamer mist carrying the two of them back from what had been the most incredible experience of her lifetime. She'd had one or two really great dates before but this one had outshone them all. She still couldn't believe that it had almost been twenty-four hours since Mark had stood in her doorway, waiting to whisk her off to never-never land.

From the moment he'd pulled his oversize SUV out of her driveway, she'd been on a pure adrenaline rush. They'd driven to the private sector of Dallas Love Field Airport. After boarding the Stallion jet for a three-hour flight to Miami they'd been picked up in South Florida by a stretch limousine. The plush luxury of the surroundings had been sensory overload at its very best.

The limo had transferred them to another section of

Miami's bustling airport where they'd boarded a jet helicopter that gave them a grand tour of Florida's inland waterways and a wealth of crystal blue ocean. Michelle was even amused as Mark gave her a who's who tour of the celebrity mansions that lined the coast. Things like that had never impressed Michelle, but there had been something infectious about Mark's enthusiasm. He hadn't been boastful, just entertaining as he'd regaled her with tales of his encounters with the rich and famous. It had been apparent that Mark didn't hang on any celebrity coattails, but his good-friend list was exceptionally long and distinguished. Mark had made her laugh like Michelle hadn't laughed in a very long time and every minute of it had felt exhilarating.

They'd landed just in time for a late-afternoon lunch of raw oysters, conch chowder and cedar-plank-roasted yellowtail fish with a basil cream sauce. The restaurant, a small noisy shack on the water had a casual, comfortable ambiance that belied the gourmet menu. Bottles of ice-chilled beer and the most delectable, melt-in-your-mouth key lime pie had capped off the meal nicely.

After Michelle had been thoroughly satiated, the two of them had chatted eagerly about their shared interests. The man had quite an entrepreneurial spirit and Michelle enjoyed hearing him talk about his accomplishments. She was equally impressed with his philanthropic activities, Mark clearly moved by being able to do for others. She could almost hear her uncle Simon whispering in her ear that a man with a giving heart was a man with a good spirit.

It quickly became apparent that despite his playboy reputation, Mark was a true romantic and Michelle realized that she could easily get used to a man who catered to her so unabashedly. Mark had left nothing to chance, conducting every nuance of their time together. Michelle loved how he opened doors and pulled out chairs for her, questioning whether or not she was enjoying every minute of their excursion and prepared to change anything that didn't meet with Michelle's approval or satisfaction. Michelle would never have thought that princess treatment could actually go very far with her, but she was definitely moved by the way he treated her like royalty.

When Mark had suggested they go snorkeling in the warm oceanic waters, Michelle had momentarily thought to remind him that she was still wearing a dress and hadn't come prepared to swim, but like magic, a two-piece tankini and snorkeling equipment appeared. Before Michelle could muster a comment the two of them had been swimming hand in hand as Michelle experienced the marine life like she'd never experienced it before.

She heaved a deep sigh, warm breath washing over her lips into the cabin's cool air. Without realizing it she had leaned her head against Mark's chest, allowing her body to snuggle close to his. She was exhausted but happy, and she was enjoying every minute of her time with the source of all that joy. Michelle felt completely at ease and it surprised the heck out of her.

Mark eased an arm around her back and shoulders and pulled her close. He'd been having an absolutely incredible time with the woman, Michelle's infectious energy fueling his own. They fit nicely together and Mark liked how well they complemented each other.

After they'd explored the coral reefs, Mark had summoned the helicopter back. His last surprise for the day even had him patting himself on the back, the event tickling Michelle like nothing else had. It had been crystal clear that she was as much an adrenaline junkie as he was, thriving on a fast and furious lifestyle. Mark knew how to do fast and furious well and he was excited to share that part of himself with a woman who could easily hold her own.

Michelle's face had brightened with excitement when their pilot had landed the helicopter next to an L-39 Russian fighter jet. That excitement had spilled out with her laughter as the flight crew had geared them both up for the ride of all rides. For almost thirty minutes the two had traveled at speeds well over five hundred miles per hour. They'd done loops, rolls and other positive G-force aerobatic maneuvers that had Michelle bubbling like a second-grader on Christmas morning.

The pilot had even allowed Michelle to briefly fly the jet herself and when all was said and finished the woman was still talking about her good time. Mark had been delirious with his own excitement, thrilled that he'd been able to pull the day off without a hitch. By the time they were done both were ready for an evening of calm and quiet and Mark had insured calm and quiet was what they got.

The friend of a friend had loaned his private island for their evening retreat. A seaplane had taken them off the coast of Florida to the exquisite hideaway where a private island boat had met them. Before Michelle could question where they were headed, the staff had prepared her second tropical island drink. Michelle was clutching its little paper umbrella in the palm of her hand, beginning to think that all of this had to be one sweet, sweet dream.

Dinner was even more sumptuous than lunch, the seaside table elegantly set against the backdrop of an exquisite sunset. The filet mignon had melted like butter and neither could remember ever having such a decadent baked potato with its lavish assortment of condiments. The meal was a solid, stick-to-your-ribs feast of all Mark's favorites and he was thrilled to learn that Michelle wasn't an organic veggie and no-meat kind of gal. Mark liked a woman who enjoyed food. He considered it an art form to eat and eat well. Michelle didn't disappoint him.

During the flight back home, the plane hit a small pocket of turbulence, causing Michelle to shift against Mark. As she tilted her head to stare up at him, it was almost as if she could see the thoughts coursing through his memory and, just like she was, he was clearly thinking about the evening they'd spent together. Michelle allowed herself to drift back into the memories.

After dinner, the duo had retreated to opposite ends of the luxurious home. Mark had grinned broadly when Michelle realized he wasn't going to try to maneuver her directly into his bed.

"Why do you look so surprised?" Mark had asked, his face gleaming beneath the dimly lit room lights.

Michelle had shrugged. "I just thought…well, it's nothing…nothing really," she said, deciding to just leave well enough alone.

Mark had laughed. "You really thought I wasn't going to be a gentleman. Didn't you?"

She smiled. "Not at all. It was just—"

Mark interrupted her, taking a broad step to stand directly in front of her. "So, tell me what it is," he said softly. "What's on your mind?"

Michelle's eyes widened, the proximity of his body shooting an electrical current straight through her. She shook the sensation and shrugged. "I just wanted to tell you what a really nice time I've had. I can't believe you did all of this."

Mark nodded his agreement. "I've had a great time as well. We'll definitely have to do it again. You will do it again with me?" he asked, his voice dropping. The seductive tone was so mesmerizing that Michelle could feel herself dropping head first into the pleasures it promised.

Michelle found herself glancing quickly about to see if any of the staff was eavesdropping on their conversation. There was no one else to be seen in the massive corridor that connected one part of the home to another. Mark was still standing so close that had anyone walked in their direction they could have easily been mistaken for one body and not two. When he'd leaned in, allowing his cheek to brush lightly against hers, Michelle had stopped breathing, air suddenly failing her at the gentle brush of his touch against her skin. As he trailed an index finger down the length of her arm, she broke out into chills, every square inch of her flesh bristling for more of his touch.

Mark had winked, taking a step back away from her. "There's a change of clothes in the back bedroom," he said casually, as if nothing had just passed between them. "Why don't you make yourself comfortable, then meet me back out on the lanai?"

Nodding her affirmation, Michelle had watched him head back down the hall from which they'd just come, turning to give her a wide grin before disappearing out of sight. Even in the air-conditioned space it had suddenly gotten hotter than she ever imagined it getting.

Moving into the luxury of the spacious bedroom, Michelle couldn't help but laugh out loud at the wardrobe Mark had laid out for her. The signature pink Victoria's Secret box held the cutest set of cotton pajamas. The cut was oversize and comfortable with a button-front top, shirt collar and front pockets. The pants were full length with a drawstring waist and elastic back. They were sleepover pajamas, Michelle thought, remembering the boy-cut garments she and her girl-friends had worn back in the day.

After a quick shower, Michelle had slipped into the pajamas and a pair of fuzzy bunny slippers. That man has some sense of humor, Michelle had thought to herself, laughing at the absurdity of the bedroom shoes, with their bunny face and floppy ears. Michelle continued to giggle back down the length of hallway.

Outside Mark sat waiting for her, dressed in his own pair of pajamas and bedroom slippers that resembled some large fuzzy animal.

Michelle rolled her eyes. She pointed toward his feet. "Bulldogs?"

"Cute, huh?" the man answered.

"You're scaring me."

Mark laughed, tossing his head back with glee. "Where's your sense of adventure, woman? These slippers should give you a sense of calm and comfort."

"Is this how you always roll?"

Mark extended his hand out for hers. "It depends on who I'm rolling with. Walk with me," he said as he gently pulled her along beside him.

Together they had strolled through the magnificent gardens, hand in hand. The moment had been simply enchanting as they'd reminisced about their day. Conversation had flowed easily between them, both finding a level of comfort with each other like neither would have imagined. Michelle marveled at just how much the two had in common, sharing interests that ran the gamut from simple board games to hot-air ballooning and skydiving. With the garden lights casting a warm glow over the environment and the sheer beauty of the surroundings inciting her senses, Michelle found herself enjoying the time more than she would ever have anticipated.

As they had strolled the length of beachfront, they'd both kicked off their slippers and had walked barefoot along the edge of the sand where the flecks of white earth kissed the clear blue water. The roar of the waves was mesmerizing and before long the two of them were racing through the incoming tide, warm water dampening the bottom of their pajama pants. Together they'd played like kids, tousling back and forth without a care in the world.

Back on the oversize patio, Mark had pulled her down beside him on an oversize lounge chair, the duo wrapping themselves into the folds of a lightweight blanket to ward off the cooling evening air.

"Can I ask you a question?" Mark said, curiosity edging his tone.

Michelle nodded. "Ask me anything you want."

"Why are you working for Greg Rockman?"

The question threw her off guard. "Why shouldn't I work for Uncle Greg? He's a great guy."

Mark bristled. "Now that's funny."

"Why?"

"Because there is nothing great about Greg Rockman. There is absolutely nothing likable about that fool."

Michelle listened as Mark went into a lengthy litany about the ills of Greg Rockman. She'd heard many of the same complaints before from others. She knew Rockman rubbed people the wrong way, his abrasive nature irking most folks he came into contact with. But ever since she'd been a little girl he'd always been kind to her, his gestures of friendship alluding to a softer side of the man that few others were privy to. She pled his case.

"I don't agree. He's been a wonderful and supportive friend. He and my father were best friends. They went way back, even before I was born, and after my dad died, he couldn't have been nicer to me," she said when Mark was finished bashing the man. "If you knew him better you'd know what I mean."

Mark shrugged. "I do know him. Well. We were business partners once. Our two companies were contracted to work on a very large project together. Rockman did some backdoor maneuvering to pump up his own profits and, subsequently, the deal went bad. It left a lot of people who'd been promised new housing out in the cold.

"Rockman profited from other folks' misfortune. He lost my respect and I'm still paying to make amends to people who'd trusted us." Mark inhaled a wealth of air and blew it past his full lips. In that single moment it dawned on him how much he truly resented Greg Rockman. He looked up to see Michelle staring at him.

She nodded slowly, not quite sure what to say if she said anything at all. She understood that business sometimes didn't go the way powers wanted it to. She still couldn't fault Rockman for something that didn't have anything at all to do with her. All she could do was reiterate everything good the man had done for her and how much she'd appreciated his gestures of goodwill.

Taking a deep breath, Mark sensed that nothing he could say about Greg Rockman would ever dissuade Michelle from believing the man was the best thing since white bread. Making a mental note to revisit the issue at a later date, Mark changed the subject to something more personal.

"Why aren't you married?" Mark had asked, his fingers still entwined between hers.

Michelle had shrugged her narrow shoulders. "I haven't found the right guy, I guess."

"And what's your right guy like?"

Michelle paused, reflecting on his question. It was on the tip of her tongue to respond, *you,* but she didn't, not bothering to say anything at all. She moved to deflect the conversation back on him. "Why don't you tell me something? Why are you still unattached?"

Mark smiled. "The right woman took her dear sweet time finding me."

Michelle nodded. "Is that so? But she's done that now as opposed to before?"

"Most definitely. She just doesn't know it yet."

Michelle could feel him staring at her, his gaze boring a hole straight through her. She refused to meet his eyes, struggling to avoid the rise of yearning that was teasing her feminine spirit with a vengeance.

"And who is this woman and why isn't she here with you right now?" Michelle ventured to ask, not sure she wanted to hear his answer.

"Who says she isn't?" Mark answered nonchalantly.

At a loss for words, Michelle just let his comment simmer in the evening air, a full moon raging above them. Wrapping his arms around her torso, he'd held her close, the two of them staring skyward to the light-filled sky. Against the dark backdrop of the crystal-clear landscape, billions of stars twinkled brightly, shimmering like gold. Time passed too quickly and before either of them had realized it, a whole hour had passed without them having shared another word. Mark's fingers had continued to dance against Michelle's arms and back, and he'd nuzzled into her neck, inhaling the scent of her. Michelle hadn't been able to resist the opportunity to take their connection to another level.

Before she realized what she was doing, Michelle turned

her body into his, reaching both of her arms around his neck as she pulled him to her. Her gaze met his just briefly before she closed her eyes tightly and leaned in to kiss his mouth. His lips fit nicely against hers, the connection teasing her senses. The moment was divine, as if it had been ordained by a power higher than either of them could have imagined.

Michelle was surprised when Mark suddenly pulled away from her, moving to his feet. She stared up at him, emotion registered on her face. "What is it?" she asked, not quite sure she wanted to hear the answer.

Mark shook his head, fighting not to meet her stare. He knew if he looked at her there would be no denying the rise of nature between his legs that had swelled full and hungry for her. He was determined that Michelle not think this trip was all about him getting her into his bed. This trip had surely turned into so much more.

"I was just thinking that I should let you go get some sleep. You've had a big day today and I imagine you might like some alone time," he answered, trying to maintain a casual tone.

Michelle raised a questioning brow. *No, actually that's not what I was wanting at all,* she thought to herself, flashes of what she had been thinking racing through her thoughts in panoramic view. She shifted her body onto her knees, lifting herself upward. She pressed her hand lightly against Mark's abdomen, her fingers tracing light circles around his belly button. "I was thinking that we might enjoy *dessert* before breakfast tomorrow," she said coyly, her bold expression surprising him.

Mark chuckled, finally allowing his eyes to meet hers. The sight of her took his breath away. Michelle was absolutely exquisite with her hair flowing softly around her face. Suddenly every muscle in his body was hard and wanting. He fought to regain some composure. "Mitch, I don't think we should be…"

Before he could finish speaking, Michelle reached up and kissed him again, her tongue gliding boldly past the line of his teeth, reaching for the back of his throat. The woman's daring incited his own and Mark couldn't resist wrapping his arms around her and pulling her close against him.

Their kiss seemed to last forever, his mouth dancing with excitement against her mouth. Rational thought seemed lost to both of them as they fell deep into the reverie of the moment. Michelle had pressed her pelvis tightly to his, grinding seductively against the rising bulge in his pajama bottoms. Unable to resist, Mark lightly pressed the palm of his hand against the round of her right breast, the gesture so unexpected that Michelle lost her breath, feeling as if the air had been knocked right out of her. When she suddenly pulled herself away from him, Mark's disappointment was acute. "I'm sorry!" he said, feeling awkward at her reaction. "I thought you…I didn't mean…"

Michelle giggled, a nervous titter that carried loudly through the midnight air. She pressed a finger to his lips. "Everything is fine, Mark. It was going very fast and feeling just a touch too good. You need to know that I'm really not this easy."

Mark laughed with her as he pressed a kiss to the palm of her hand. "I never thought you were easy, baby. But I was certainly enjoying the moment. I like it when a woman takes control," he said, his voice dropping to a low, seductive drone. "I like it very much."

Michelle could feel herself blushing profusely, color flooding her cheeks. "Why don't we take another walk," she suggested, rising from her seat.

Mark stood with her, clasping her hand beneath his own as they headed back down to the beach.

Silence swelled full and thick between them. The moment was easy and comfortable and Michelle couldn't begin to imagine herself having a better time. She sensed that Mark was feeling the same way. Hand in hand the two strolled slowly back to the beach, pausing to stare out toward the dark, star-filled sky. At the ocean's edge, Michelle sat down on the sand, pulling Mark down beside her. The sea lapped gently at them, occasionally racing up and covering their naked feet before pulling back out into the depths of darkness around them.

Mark turned to face her, the glow of the moon above illuminating his view. "You are so beautiful," he started, his tone serious.

Michelle smiled at him. "Thank you," she said softly, nudging him affectionately. "So are you!"

Mark chuckled warmly, wrapping an arm around her shoulders. He leaned to kiss her one more time as Michelle placed both her hands on either side of his face, gently meeting his mouth with her own. She was soft and sweet and his erection surged fuller than ever before. He wanted her. He wanted her badly and everything in him told him Michelle wanted him as much, her kiss increasing fiercely.

When Michelle slipped her tongue between his lips, Mark became lost in the moment, moaning softly. Both were breathing deeply, senses suddenly buzzing out of control. Michelle knew there would be no turning back and nothing within her wanted to. She pulled away, rising to her feet.

Mark eyed her curiously, his gaze questioning why she'd stopped for a second time.

"I need to wash off some of this sand," Michelle said matter-of-factly. She extended her hand in his direction.

As Mark stood beside her, Michelle leaned to kiss him again, pressing her body tight against his. Before Mark realized what was happening the woman had slipped a warm hand past the elastic in his pajama bottoms, her palm wrapping around his manhood as she caressed him gently.

"Then we need to do something about this," Michelle whispered softly.

Mark gasped as she slowly stroked him, every nerve ending in his body beginning to quiver with anticipation. As quickly as Michelle had touched him, she stopped and headed back toward the exquisite homestead. Mark followed like a lovesick puppy behind her, the woman of his dreams in complete and total control.

Back inside, Michelle paused for just a quick minute, her gaze skating from one hallway to the other. Mark laughed as he pointed toward his bedroom, trailing along beside Michelle as she led the way. When the bedroom door was closed behind them, securing them from view, the woman's intent became crystal clear.

With a strength Mark didn't expect, Michelle pushed him gently down against the bed, reaching to link her hands above his head as she straddled his body. As she kissed him with a fierce determination, Mark responded hungrily. Michelle pressed herself hard against him as he ran his fingers up and down the length of her back.

"I want you so much right now," Michelle whispered when they finally came up for air. "You won't think badly of me, will you?" she asked, meeting his gaze.

Before Mark could respond, her mouth was clinging to his. Her hand moved across his pajama top, pulling at the short row of buttons that kept it closed. Pushing the garment off his shoulders, Michelle paused as he sat up just enough to pull his arms free, wrapping them around her. An audible moan rushed past his lips as Michelle's fingers brushed a bold trail across his chest, lightly pinching one hardened nipple and then the other.

Mark ran a thick finger down the woman's cheek until he reached her bottom lip. Before Michelle realized what had happened, Mark had rolled her onto her back, unbuttoning her shirt. His eyes never left hers, the man feeling like he was unwrapping a long-awaited present. As she lay naked from the waist up Mark drank in the sight of her bare breasts. Michelle was stunning and he said so.

Michelle laughed softly as Mark planted a series of delicate kisses along the length of her neck and in the hollow of her collarbone. When he leaned to wrap his lips around her right nipple, suckling one and then the other, Michelle trembled beneath him. His tongue bathed her with affection as it danced in a lazy, circular motion against the lush tissue. Michelle heard herself moan his name, unable to contain the wave of emotion that had consumed her.

Mark moved his hands to her waist, pushing at the sleeping pants that still covered her. When her pants were sitting around her knees, he slowly stroked the inside of her thighs, admiring the lacy black panties beneath her garments. His touch burned hot against her skin as Michelle's breathing became ragged.

Moisture dampened every crease and crevice of Michelle's body. She was wet with wanting, her panties soaked as Mark ran a finger beneath the elastic leg of her undergarment. Lifting himself above her, Mark pushed her clothes past her ankles and onto the floor. Stepping out of his own clothes, he stood staring down at her as Michelle reached a hand out to pull him back to her.

Moving back onto the bed, Mark positioned one knee between her legs and pushed it gently against her crotch. Michelle spread herself open and began thrusting her hips against the man. Moving in sync, the two fell into a gentle, erotic rhythm with each other. Mark leaned back down, returning his mouth to hers as they shared a long, passionate kiss. Mark felt her pelvic muscles contract against his leg as Michelle suddenly gasped out loud, her body arching upward off the bed.

"Oh, yes," she hissed, her hands clutching the bedsheets beneath them. Her eyes were shining brightly as she stared up at him. Mark nodded as he lay against her, planting butterfly kisses along her shoulders. He kissed the side of her neck, his tongue tiptoeing into her ear. Michelle wrapped her legs around his buttocks, her arms clutching at his back.

"Again!" she whispered, the word commanding Mark's full attention.

Pulling away from her, the man crossed over to the other side of the room, searching inside his overnight bag. Seconds later he returned to her side with a wrapped condom in his hand. Michelle watched as he rolled the prophylactic around his raging erection. Mark was hard as steel and she reached for him, grabbing him boldly.

The two lay side by side, staring at each other. Lingering gazes clearly detailed what both were thinking. Michelle suddenly felt completely lost in the sweeping depths of the man's haunting gaze and the brilliance of his overwhelming smile. A curious sensation prickled at her navel and her breath shortened, gasps of air coming in deep, short pants. Mark seemed to feel what she was feeling as he pressed his palm to the flat of her stomach and slowly leaned in to capture her mouth beneath his own.

Michelle couldn't begin to deny her surging desire as she kissed him back, her longing for the man having shifted into an intense hunger. Wrapping her arms around him, she pulled him close, savoring the sensation of heat that had risen like a thick flame between them. His tongue danced in the moist cavity of her mouth, two-stepping with her own. He tasted like dark chocolate and strawberries, remnants of the decadent treat the two had shared.

Mark was overcome with emotion he'd never experienced before. Holding Michelle in his arms felt like the most natural thing for him to do. He imagined they were the only two in the world, everyone and everything else no longer existing. He'd been determined that Michelle wouldn't think this trip was just his way of fulfilling some sexual fantasy, but right there, in that moment, all he wanted was to make love to her. Mark had never truly made love to any woman before, his previous connections just moments of sexual release for him and a partner. He was desperate for Michelle to understand this moment was about so much more for him.

"Mitch, baby, I..." Mark stammered, words lost deep in his chest. Tears welled in his eyes, brimming at the edge of his lashes.

Michelle stared into the gulf of desire that beckoned her closer. She was giddy, intoxicated with desire. Her own tears rolled off her cheek and Mark moved to kiss them away. She nodded her head with understanding, and then Mark pressed himself into her, melding his body into hers.

The moment was surreal as they moved one against the other. Naked flesh burned hot against naked flesh as Mark pushed and pulled himself in and out of her, Michelle meeting him stroke for stroke. And then Mark cried out her name, the lull of it rolling off his tongue again and again as waves of pleasure washed over the two of them.

Michelle jumped out of the trance of memory, the jet suddenly shifting directions in the deep blue sky. Mark tightened his grip around her, his fingers entwined with hers.

"Mitch, is everything okay?" he asked, concern spilling out of his words.

Michelle nodded her head. "I'm fine. I was just thinking about…" She paused, knowing that there was no need for her to tell him what she'd been thinking about. The memories of their time together hadn't left either of them behind.

Every muscle in her body still tingled from the experience. Michelle couldn't get over how she'd gotten caught up in the moment, every rational thought failing her. The two of them had made love over and over again, sleep eluding them for most of the night, and even as the sun rose, welcoming the new day, the duo had been invigorated enough to make love to each other one more time.

Mark smiled, a warm grin filling his dark face. "So was I," he said softly. "So was I."

The moment was interrupted by the stewardess, who approached with a tray of fresh fruit in hand.

"Mr. Stallion, the pilot says we'll be landing in another hour. May I get anything for either of you?"

Mark looked toward Michelle, who shook her head. "No, I think we're both fine, thank you," he answered.

The woman smiled, depositing the fruit tray on the table in front of them before making her way back to the galley of the plane. Michelle sighed, then curled herself against Mark as she fell back into thought.

The two had eventually drifted off to sleep, wrapped warmly in each other's arms as they'd traded light caresses, and when they'd finally woken, a midmorning sun greeting them, they'd still been locked in an embrace.

Just like Mark had promised, breakfast had been equally divine, a crystal-clear day beaming over the horizon as they'd sipped on pineapple mimosas and dined on fresh omelets made right there at their table, laughing over one story after another. The two had spent the rest of the afternoon talking, sharing everything they could think to share with each other.

Michelle learned that Mark wanted a large family, all boys, never considering that he might ever have daughters. Michelle had never imagined herself the mother of a boy or a girl and suddenly she was thinking what it might be like to mother Mark Stallion's babies. Michelle could not imagine any moment ever having been more perfect.

Michelle still couldn't begin to figure out what had gotten into her, but whatever it was had her feeling on top of the world. She hadn't felt this good in a long time. She heaved a deep sigh as Mark leaned to press a warm kiss to her forehead. One more hour before landing, she thought, then her fairy-tale adventure would come to an end and Mitch the mechanic would have to go back to the everyday routine of her life.

Chapter 11

Mark's frustration was rampant as he pulled into the Briscoe-Stallion homestead. It had been well over a week since his weekend tryst with Michelle and he'd not heard one word from her. As he shut down the engine of his car and sat staring out the window, he thought back to the last conversation they'd had as he'd walked her to her door. Michelle had thanked him for their good time together and then she'd kissed him sweetly on the cheek, promising to give him a call.

"Maybe we can have dinner tomorrow?" Mark had asked, hopeful.

Michelle's smile had been sugar sweet. "I'm sorry but I have plans," she'd answered.

Mark had nodded enthusiastically. "Well, why don't I call you on Monday and we can make plans to do something during the week."

"Let's just play it by ear. I'll give you a call when I get

some free time. Okay? And, thanks again, Mark. I really enjoyed myself," she'd said as she'd reached to kiss his cheek one last time.

Mark had walked away feeling as if he'd been dismissed. He still couldn't shake the sensation and Michelle hadn't bothered to call him. He made his way to the front door of the oversize home, shaking his head. Although it was still very early in the morning, he knew that one person in particular would already be up and moving in the large home. As Mark had expected, Edward Briscoe answered the front door, welcoming him inside. "Good morning, Mark. How are you doing, son?"

Mark embraced the patriarch warmly. "Good morning, Edward. And, I'm doing okay. I guess."

Something in Mark's voice caught Edward's attention. "That doesn't sound convincing, son. You sure about that?"

Mark shrugged. "Just a lot on my mind, sir. I was hoping to catch you alone. I could use some advice."

Edward gestured for Mark to follow him into the kitchen and family room. "Well, let's see what kind of help I can offer," Edward said casually. "What's got you down? A woman, or a woman?"

Mark chuckled warmly. "Is it that obvious?"

Edward nodded. "I heard about that mess you got in at Marah's thing the other week. It didn't sound pretty. Those girls of mine haven't stopped talking about it—or you—since."

Mark shook his head. "No, sir, it definitely wasn't pretty."

"So, your lady friend still isn't speaking with you, huh?"

Mark let out a deep sigh. "I don't know what's going on," Mark said, confusion washing over his expression. He took a moment to tell the older man about him and Michelle spending time together. "And I haven't heard anything from her since," Mark concluded.

Edward laughed. "Sounds like you're getting a taste of your own medicine."

Mark winced, thinking of the many women over the years that he'd promised to call and hadn't. "But this is different. This…this…" Mark stammered, not quite sure he could explain what this was.

Edward shook his own head. "It's different all right. This time it's happening to you and it doesn't feel so nice."

Mark sighed. "No, sir, it doesn't."

Edward moved to the stove top and a cast-iron frying pan he'd been heating up. "I'm cooking steak and eggs this morning. Won't you stay and have some?"

"Thank you," Mark said, shifting against the stool he'd taken a seat on. "So, what do you think I should do, Edward?" Mark asked.

There was a pregnant pause as Edward didn't respond, his attention centered on the Angus beef steaks he'd pulled from the stainless-steel refrigerator. Mark waited patiently, anxious for some sage advice.

When Edward finally spoke, Mark wasn't expecting what the man had to say. "So, why haven't you called her?" he asked casually, not bothering to look in Mark's direction.

"Excuse me?"

"Why haven't you called her? You're here pouting about her not calling you, but why haven't you called her?" Edward repeated.

Mark paused briefly before answering. "Well, she said she would call me and, well…" He paused a second time, realizing he didn't have an answer, and definitely not one that made an ounce of sense.

"So you wanted to speak with her and you sat around waiting for her to call instead of you calling her first?"

"Well, yes."

"And, now you're upset because you haven't spoken to her?"

"But she said she would call me." Mark could hear the hint of a whine in his voice and a wave of embarrassment swept through him.

Edward chuckled. "You young boys think you know it all and y'all don't know much of anything. She's still a woman and you're still the man and women like a man to chase just a little. Just because she said she'd call didn't mean you couldn't or shouldn't call her."

Mark nodded slowly. "I just didn't want…"

"What? You didn't want to talk to her."

"No, I did, but…"

"Then call her. It's not hard, son. Just pick up the phone and dial."

Feeling foolish, Mark sighed, blowing warm air past his lips.

As he did, Edward turned and tossed him a quick look. "And I suggest you call her soon 'cause I don't doubt that she's spitting bullets right about now, upset that she hasn't heard from you," he said calmly, turning back to his cooking eggs.

Confusion washed over Mark's expression. This was starting to get difficult and he wasn't used to any relationship being difficult. He was totally fascinated by the woman. Michelle had completely captivated him and here he was imagining the kind of future he could have with her. There was an air of mystery about her and then she had this bold, brash side that kept surprising him beyond his wildest dreams. He loved that she carried herself without a hint of vanity, seeming to be clueless at how much of an exquisite beauty she was.

It suddenly dawned on Mark that if he could ever imagine himself falling in love with any woman, he could easily fall in love with a woman just like Michelle. He heaved another deep sigh, blowing a gust of breath so heavily that Edward turned to give him a quick look.

"It's not that bad, son. You young boys need to stop trying to one-up your women and everything will smooth right out. You like this woman. Let her know. If you want to talk to her, call. It sounds like she likes you, too, but both of you are trying to see who's going to make the first move."

"What move? Who's moving?" Marah questioned, making her way into the room. She leaned to kiss her father's cheek. "Good morning, Daddy. Hey, Mark," she said, moving to give her brother-in-law a hug. "What are you two talking about?"

Edward said nothing, turning his attention back to his frying pan. Mark shrugged his shoulders. "I was just telling your dad about Mitch."

Marah nodded. "So how's that working for you? You make up for being an ass yet?"

The man tossed her a look of annoyance. "Yes, I made up for that ill-timed moment. And I thought she'd forgiven me."

"You thought? What's the problem now?" Marah questioned, pouring herself a cup of hot coffee from the pot on the counter. She moved to the stool next to Mark and sat down.

Mark eyed Edward before settling his gaze back on Marah's curious face. "It's just not going how I imagined it would."

"You need to show her some old-fashioned romance."

"Old-fashioned? I thought I was romancing her," Mark said, sharing select details of their weekend away.

"Not bad for starters," Marah mused, "but you need to take it to a whole other level. I'm sure Mitch had a great time, but that just fed every rumor she's ever heard about your womanizing ways. You need to approach this from a whole other angle." Marah tipped her head in his direction as she sipped from her coffee cup. "If you need some advice I'm always open for business," she concluded.

Mark crossed his arms over his chest. Behind them, the aroma of grilled steak was rising in the room, teasing the air around them. Mark took a deep breath of the decadent aroma as he mulled over his sister-in-law's comments. "So," he asked finally, "how much is this advice going to cost me?" Mark queried, eyeing Marah with a hint of reservation.

Marah gave him a big grin back. "Not to worry, brother dear. You're going to get the family discount."

Simon ducked as Michelle threw a wrench from one side of the garage to the other. "Hey, what's the matter with you?" the old man said, his tone scolding. "That was my head you almost took off!"

Michelle's frustration blanketed her face. "Sorry about that, Uncle Simon. I'm just…well…it's like…"

Simon nodded. "Yeah, Mitch, that does sound really bad."

Michelle rolled her eyes skyward. "Did anyone call for me?" she asked, shifting her weight from one hip to the other.

"Yeah, some guy called."

Michelle's eyes widened excitedly. "What guy?"

Simon shrugged. "Don't know. He didn't leave his name. Just wanted to know if you thought he had the word *stupid* tattooed on his forehead."

The young woman looked confused. "Excuse me?"

Simon grinned. "Just like I figured it out, don't you think everyone else can figure it out, too? You're back here throwing a fuss 'cause that Stallion boy ain't called you yet!"

Michelle tossed her hands up into the air. "You don't know what you're talking about, Uncle Simon. I'm not thinking about that man."

Simon laughed, tapping his index figure against his forehead. "I must got *stupid* across my forehead, too!"

Michelle turned from where she stood, dropping to the ground to crawl beneath a car that needed her attention. In the distance she could hear Simon still laughing warmly as he made his way back to the office. Hearing the door close behind the old man, Michelle moved from where she was, clearing the undercarriage of the car. She shifted her body until she was able to sit upright, leaning her back against the vehicle's door.

She'd been too nervous to call Mark, believing that he wouldn't have been expecting her call in the first place. Of course she had been hoping Mark would have just reached out and called her first and, when he hadn't, she'd begun to question her behavior. She'd surely not gone out with the man wanting him to think that she would fall into his bed. And when she'd behaved so wantonly, wanting him like she'd never wanted any man before, she'd become scared.

Taking that next step, instead of cooling the rise of emotions between them, had left her feeling completely out of control and it was that flood of emotions that had consumed her like nothing she'd ever experienced before. And then confusion about what had happened between them had rushed in to cloud the clarity in her head.

Everyone knew Mark Stallion didn't do forever with any woman and Michelle had found herself wishing for forever. She'd thoroughly enjoyed that side of him that Mark had exposed—his vulnerability, compassion and spirit fulfilling every wish she'd ever had for a partner. And then she found herself remembering once again that Mark didn't do forever. A cold chill caressed her spine.

After their tryst, Michelle hadn't been sure what would

happen between them, believing the time they'd spent together could actually have just been a one-time thing. And although Mark hadn't done anything to provoke the emotion, Michelle had found herself feeling like she could potentially be just a notch in the man's very lengthy tool belt. Petrified that Mark might not have been quite as interested in her as she was finding herself interested in him had fueled more doubt and kept her from reaching out to him.

It truly wasn't her nature to jump into a physical relationship with any man and jumping with Mark so quickly had Michelle doing things she would never have imagined herself ever doing. In her mind she'd clearly pushed the limits of that first-date etiquette and ever since then she'd been waiting for a telephone call that said she was wrong, a telephone call that hadn't come, and she'd been too nervous and a touch embarrassed to even think about calling him first.

Michelle let the smell of new rubber tires fill her lungs. Maybe she should just call him and get it over with, she thought. Clearly, if the man wasn't interested he'd let her know pretty quickly. Michelle reached into the inner pocket of her coveralls for her cell phone. Staring at the device for a split second, she suddenly found herself with a pretty pair of very cold feet. Shaking her head lightly, she tucked the phone back into her pocket and moved to look under the hood of the vehicle she'd been working on. Maybe later, she thought. Maybe she'd get up the nerve to call Mark sometime later.

Greg Rockman had a knack for stirring up trouble and the commotion brewing through the driver's circuit was just a small example of his handiwork. He took great pleasure in knowing that the right words whispered into the wrong ears could sweep from team to team faster than if a group of grade-school girls were playing a game of telephone at a slumber party. Greg had whispered and gossip was flying fast and furious.

He feigned a compassionate smile in Michelle's direction, lifting a hand to give her a slight wave. Acknowledging him with a nod of her head, Michelle turned back to the bike she was tuning up, her attention focused on the complaints the bike's rider was listing in detail. A group gathered across the way was eyeing Michelle as well, the men staring blatantly as they muttered back and forth. With a satisfied expression pasted on his face, Rockman turned on his heels to head back to the parking lot and his silver-gray Cadillac.

Michelle heard the secondhand gossip from the twentieth or thirtieth person to pass it along. Everyone was whispering that she might have had something to do with the number of accidents that seemed to be plaguing the racetrack, Jack Crenshaw's driver being the latest victim. Ric, the mechanic who'd come to pass the news along, hadn't realized Michelle had been standing behind him as he'd whispered his version of the tall tale to the team of men listening. He wasn't too happy when Michelle made her presence known.

"Who's saying I jacked up Bill Bob's engine?" Michelle had exclaimed, tension rising in her tone.

The tall Asian man with the deep caramel tan suddenly looked flustered as he spun around in her direction. "Sorry, Mitch. I didn't see you there," Ric stammered nervously.

Michelle nodded. "So, who's saying it? Because I never touched that man's ride." She moved in his direction, stopping directly in front of him.

"It's just going around. Folks just have some questions is all."

"What kinds of questions?"

"Well, Purdue says you were in his garage before his driver

lost the lug nuts to his ride and Michael Mann claims you helped Joe Dooley work on his bike right before his accident."

"I didn't work on Dooley's bike. He asked me a question about his engine and I answered it. My contract doesn't allow me to work on any other competitor's bike. You know that. And why would I do something like that? Dooley and Mann were both hurt badly. Why would I want something like that to happen to either of them?"

There was barely a sound to be heard as everyone stood staring at Michelle, no one bothering to respond. Michelle looked from one man to the other, her gaze insisting on an answer.

Ric glanced quickly over his shoulder, wishing he could run and hide. Michelle's stare was pressing for a response and he couldn't figure out a way to disappear from Michelle's sight. He heaved a deep sigh. "Sorry, Mitch. It's just that folks is wondering whether or not you might have a grudge about what happened to your father. You know how it is."

The woman dropped her hands to her waist, distress rising to furrow her brow. "No, Ric, I don't know how it is. But I do know how it shouldn't be. You guys know me better than that. I don't know where this is coming from so it definitely shouldn't be like this."

The silence was suddenly deafening, no one bothering to say a thing. Michelle finally nodded her head. "I didn't have anything to do with any of their accidents," she said, her tone drifting back to normal. "I would hope that you all would know that."

The man shrugged. "I know, Mitch. I was just repeating what I heard."

"Well, don't."

Slinking back in the direction he'd come from, the man had

looked nervously back over his shoulder at Michelle and the harsh expression that had crossed her face. The men around her had tried to be comforting, assuring her that it was nothing but talk that would soon go away.

Michelle had wanted to believe them, and then she'd been summoned up to the offices to meet with the tracks owners, their attorney and a team of detectives from the local police force, and Michelle realized nothing was very much something after all.

Chapter 12

Michelle was ranting as she paced back and forth from one end of Rockman's office to the other. The man was sitting behind his large oak desk, his hands clasped as if in prayer on the desktop. He was nodding his head sympathetically as Michelle bemoaned her latest woes.

"I'm sure this is going to blow over very soon, Mitch," he said, his words less than comforting.

Michelle shook her head, slouching down onto a seat in front of him. "I can't believe they actually questioned me, Uncle Greg. You know I'd never do anything to hurt a driver like that. Someone did that to my father. I know what the repercussions can be."

Rockman cringed, avoiding Michelle's gaze as he spun around in his seat. Voiding his face of any emotion, he turned back to face her. "Michelle, dear, I understand what you're saying. I know you couldn't have possibly done what they're accusing you of. You know you have my full support."

Michelle nodded, the length of her hair swaying around her face. "Thank you." She blew a deep sigh. "They didn't ask this many questions when my father crashed. Why wasn't his case investigated as thoroughly?"

"Mitch, they did investigate. What happened to your father was unfortunate."

Michelle bristled and then snapped. "What happened to my father shouldn't have happened at all. I checked his bike that morning myself. There was nothing wrong with my father's bike. Nothing. Someone sabotaged him. I just know it!" Michelle suddenly sat upright. "Uncle Greg, do you think whoever cut my father's brake line could be responsible for all these other accidents?"

She eyed the man anxiously, hoping that her father's friend would see the conspiracy theory she'd just fathomed. Instead, Rockman rose quickly from his seat, moving to the decanter of Scotch that he kept on the counter in the room as he ignored her question. "Would you like a drink?" he asked as he poured the caramel-colored fluid into a shot glass. "It might take the edge off."

Michelle shook her head no. "Thank you, but I really don't drink, sir." She blew another sigh. "I'm just so frustrated. I've been asking questions and no one seems to know anything and now when there are other accidents happening, everyone wants to point a finger at me." Michelle's voice dropped softly as she fought back a sudden urge to cry. "It's just not fair. It's not fair at all."

Rockman downed his drink in one gulp and poured himself another. "No, dear, it isn't. But I promise you everything is going to be just fine. You just trust me, okay?"

Michelle lifted her mouth into a slight smile. "Yes, sir, Uncle Greg. I'm sorry to bother you with all this. You've been so good to me and…"

Rockman moved to Michelle's side, pressing a sweaty palm against her bare arm. "You know I would do anything for you, Mitch. Anything. You're very special to me. Always have been."

Michelle smiled again. "I know. You were a good friend to my father and you've been a great friend to me. I hope you know how much I appreciate everything you've done."

Nodding, Rockman grinned. The man leaned to press his lips to Michelle's forehead, and then her cheek, his beard tickling her flesh. She giggled softly. He held the kiss just a second longer than necessary, turning nervously when Michelle pulled away from him.

As Michelle said her goodbyes, Rockman rushed back behind his desk, reaching for the telephone. He dialed quickly, waiting for an answer on the other end. Seconds later a man's voice answered.

Rockman hissed into the receiver. "It's starting to look like I might have a serious problem. If you want to keep your job then I suggest you make that problem go away fast!"

Flowers were sitting in wait at the threshold of Michelle's front door when she arrived home that evening. It was a beautiful bouquet of yellow roses and Peruvian lilies in a simple glass vase tied with a large bow. At the sight of them Michelle found herself smiling, curious to know who had sent her flowers. Picking the arrangement up off the floor, Michelle pushed her key into the door lock and eased herself inside. Setting the flowers atop her kitchen counter, she pulled the small gift card into her hand, anxious to see who'd sent her flowers.

Her curiosity was further aroused as she read the short inscription printed on the crisp white paper. *Hope you had a pleasant day. Your secret admirer.* Michelle couldn't begin to image who was secretly admiring her. Before she had time to ponder the question, her doorbell rang harshly, someone anxious to get her attention.

Moving back across the room, Michelle glanced out through the peephole, surprise sweeping from her head to her toe. Mark Stallion stood on the other side, his arms behind his back, his expression blank as he waited for her to answer. Michelle took a quick glance in the foyer mirror, wanting to kick herself for not bringing something to change into after her afternoon in the garage. She was still in her coveralls, grease and oil staining the front of her attire. Taking a deep breath and then a second, she pulled the door open and greeted the man warmly.

"Mark, what are you doing here?"

Mark Stallion flashed her a brilliant smile. "Hi. I hope you don't mind me stopping by like this."

Michelle shook her head. "Not at all. Please, come on inside."

Easing past her, Mark leaned to kiss her cheek, squeezing her arm gently beneath his palm. "What happened to you giving me a call?"

Caught off guard, Michelle stammered nervously. "I…well…I meant to…"

Mark chuckled warmly. "Don't sweat it. I should have called you," he said matter-of-factly. "I was hoping we could make it up to each other. Will you have dinner with me tonight? Do you have any plans?"

Michelle's head shook, moving with a mind of its own. "No, I don't. I really hadn't thought about dinner," she answered, finally able to complete a coherent sentence.

Mark smiled, the gesture shining brightly from his eyes. "Well, I'd really like it if you had dinner with me tonight. Nothing fancy. I thought we'd just grab a burger and fries somewhere."

"I'd like that. I'd like that a lot."

Mark moved in the direction of her kitchen, easing his way to sit on one of the bar stools that rested in front of the granite countertop. The arrangement of flowers caught his eye and he leaned to sniff the sweet aroma wafting off the roses. "These are nice. Is it your birthday?"

Michelle shook her head. "No. I don't know who sent them or why."

Mark eyed her curiously as she gestured with the gift card in her hand. "You don't know who sent you flowers?"

She shrugged, her narrow shoulders gliding upward. "It says they're from my secret admirer."

Mark's eyes widened. "Do I have some competition I need to be aware of, Ms. Coleman?"

Michelle laughed. "Do you, Mr. Stallion?"

Mark leaned in to sniff the roses one more time. "I certainly hope not," he exclaimed, his cheery expression warming. "I certainly hope not."

Michelle smiled with him. "I just need to change my clothes," she said. "Make yourself at home," she said, moving down the narrow hall toward her bedroom.

Mark called after her. "Mitch?"

Turning back to face him, Michelle eyed him curiously. "Yes?"

His voice was low, the tone seductive as he stared right into the depths of her soul. "I've really been missing you."

A current of heat did a quick flip in Michelle's stomach. With words caught deep in her throat, she didn't bother to respond, turning instead to head down the hallway. The man had left her speechless and all she could manage to do was race to hide behind the security of her locked door.

Hours later the two were resting on the lawn of the Kimball Art Museum enjoying a leisurely picnic meal of chili hot dogs, cold French fries and bottles of orange soda. Michelle couldn't believe that time had passed so quickly since they'd left her apartment, Mark guiding her first to Fort Worth's celebrated cultural area to tour the concrete, glass and aluminum structure of the Museum of Modern Art. The exquisite building had been extremely romantic with its acre and a half of water space that surrounded two sides of the building. The collections on display had been enlightening and both had enjoyed the time discussing which pieces they liked and which they didn't.

The Kimball Art Museum was situated directly across the street, and when they'd seen all the art either was interested in seeing they'd strolled through the outdoor gardens of the Kimball to take in the water fountains and rest atop a blanket Mark had acquired as if by magic.

As they'd walked and talked, the man had held her hand tightly beneath his, the warmth of his touch heating every nerve ending in Michelle's body. She couldn't believe that just days before she'd been thinking the worst of him, certain that what she'd been feeling the week before had simply been a fluke. Her expression was telling as Mark sat watching her.

"Care to share?" he asked, raising his bottle of soda to take a sip.

Michelle blushed with color, a warmth of red rising to her cheeks. "Excuse me?"

"Would you like to share what you were just thinking a moment ago?"

She smiled sweetly. "It was nothing."

"No, it was something. I could see it all over your face."

Michelle tossed him a quick glance, and then she looked away, her eyes skating everywhere except across his face. She had been thinking. The afternoon's events had been on her mind. It had just been a hair shy of being an inquisition and Michelle still wasn't feeling comfortable about the questions that had been asked of her.

She couldn't begin to fathom how anyone would think she'd purposely hurt any other person and especially not the friends who had been like family to her and her father. Replaying everything that had been said kept creeping into her mind and she'd not wanted her concerns to dampen the mood with Mark. With luck, she thought, all of this mess would just be a bad dream, gone before she realized it. She shrugged her shoulders and said nothing, grateful that Mark didn't push her for more.

Sensing her discomfort, Mark lifted her chin. When he was certain that he had her full attention, he smiled sweetly, his thumb and index finger lightly caressing her chin and cheek. "When you're ready," he said easily. "I want you to be comfortable so when you're ready just remember that you can talk to me about anything. Okay?"

Michelle nodded, knowing that she didn't need to say anything else. The two sat staring into each other's eyes, the young woman feeling as if she was falling deep into the depths of his gaze.

"I didn't think I'd ever see you again. Not like this," she said, breaking the moment of silence that had swelled full and heavy between them.

He nodded. "I didn't think you wanted to see me again."

"I apologize for that," Michelle said as she reclined back against Mark's chest, her body melding effortlessly against his broad frame. Mark moved to wrap his arms around her torso. He hugged her to his chest, pulling her to lean her head against his shoulder. "Never apologize for what you're feeling. Just don't shut me out."

She looked up into his face. "That's part of my problem, Mark. I'm not sure what I'm feeling. I've never experienced anything like this before."

Mark nodded his understanding. "Neither have I, but I like it. Whatever is happening between us feels really good."

"Yes, it does," Michelle whispered softly. "It feels very good."

Mark brushed his lips against her forehead, kissing her softly. "So, let's you and I try this again. I'm not seeing anyone else, Ms. Coleman. And I'd like very much if you and I could start dating to see if this can go anyplace. Are you interested?"

Michelle giggled softly. "Yes, sir, I am. I'm very interested."

Mark let out a loud whoop, his thick voice carrying in the cooling air. "Baby girl, you've just made me one very happy man!" he exclaimed excitedly.

His enthusiasm flooding through her, Michelle leaned back against him. A blanket of warmth spread heat straight through her as she gave in to the sensation, relishing the strength of palm and fingers that slowly massaged a path across her arms and torso. The extraordinary man had incredible hands, firm appendages that felt as if they were setting all of her nerve endings on fire. Michelle suppressed the sudden urge to moan, trying to fight the rise of wanting that threatened to consume her. It suddenly became way too much for her to bear.

Shifting her body forward, she pulled away from him, needing to break the heated connection that had her wanting her naked flesh against his naked flesh. Mark trailed his index finger over her cheek. "Are you comfortable?" he asked softly, the concern in his tone drawing her body back to his.

Michelle nodded. "I'm probably a little too comfortable," she admitted, the reality of the situation between them solidifying in her head and her heart. Mark nodded his understanding, not needing to answer.

He was feeling it as well. It was a level of comfort he'd never experienced before. Michelle made him feel like he was home, safe and secure, and when she was cradled in his arms he wanted to make everything right between them. He was quickly discovering that even the briefest time they spent together made him crave more time with her. She made him smile and there was a newfound joy that filled his spirit when they were in each other's company. He liked the woman. He liked her a lot and Mark had never felt for any woman what he was feeling for Michelle.

He kissed her cheek, allowing his lips to rest against the warmth of her caramel complexion. He took a deep breath, fighting to stall the rise of wanting that had washed over him, the wealth of it rolling like thunder through his abdomen and down into his groin.

Michelle tilted her head up, shifting her body around to face his. She leaned in slowly, her eyes shifting over his face as he smiled down at her and then she kissed him, brushing her lips gingerly to his lips. Mark inhaled the warmth of her breath as he tasted the sweetness of milk and honey. The sensual moment between them was almost intoxicating and, before either could resist, they were both breathing heavy with wanting.

"You have the most exquisite mouth," Mark exclaimed a moment later as he pulled his fingers through the length of her hair.

Michelle purred, leaning back against her shoulders, her eyes closed tight. "Hmm. So do you."

Mark chuckled, wrapping his arms tightly around her small frame. "I love kissing your mouth," he said, pressing his lips back to hers.

Michelle swooned and before she could catch control of herself, the single thought that had just crossed her mind, spilled past her lips. "I love you, too."

The simple statement had surprised Michelle more than it had surprised Mark. He'd been feeling it before she'd gotten up the nerve to say it out loud. They were falling in love with each other. It had been as crystal to him as the look of astonishment that had crossed her face when those three words had slipped unexpectedly out of her mouth.

Michelle had tried to play the moment off, nervous laughter ringing through the air. "Kissing you! I love kissing you, too!" she'd exclaimed excitedly.

Mark had laughed with her, embracing her tightly and then the two of them had changed the subject, smoothing over the emotions that had combusted like a ticking time bomb between them. It had been a great time and neither one of them had wanted to see the evening end when it had.

Mark rolled over onto his stomach, tucking one of the many pillows that filled his bed beneath his chin and arms. Thinking about Michelle was suddenly consuming every waking moment. He went to bed thinking about her. He woke up thinking about her. Most nights he spent dreaming about her as well.

No woman had ever consumed him the way Michelle was consuming him. The emotions he was feeling were foreign to everything he'd ever known in his lifetime. In his previous relationships Mark had run and run fast from the emotions he was now feeling. And now he found himself wanting to fight and fight hard for what Michelle might be in his life. Mark didn't have a clue where fate was going to take the two of them but he was hopeful for a very happy ending.

Hours later he was still wide awake, still trying to gain some control and perspective on the dance he and Michelle seemed to be doing with each other. He slid his long legs off the side of his bed, planting his large feet firmly on the floor. Moving from his bed to the hallway outside his bedroom door, Mark headed down the stairs in the direction of the kitchen.

The house was exceptionally quiet, no one but him, his brother Luke and a handful of necessary staff occupying the immense space. The magnificent Preston Hollow estate on Audubon Avenue had been the home he'd shared with his brothers since forever. Years after the death of their parents, his big brother John had built a successful business that had afforded them the luxurious property.

Constructed of Austin stone with copper accents and a tile roof, the European-style residence easily encompassed some fifteen thousand square feet of living space. It sat on some sizable acreage as well, with an expanse of landscaping that boasted a putting green, an Olympic-size swimming pool and tennis courts. But for the first time Mark was feeling very lonely in the space he called home.

Finding his way to the kitchen, he stood staring into the stainless-steel refrigerator. Dressed in nothing but a pair of boxer briefs, the air was cool against his bare skin. For a brief moment he thought about going back upstairs for his bathrobe, but he didn't imagine anyone else would be up to see him standing almost naked in the middle of the room.

Inside the refrigerator, all of his and Luke's favorites were lined neatly on the row of shelves. Between the personal chef and the housekeeper there was absolutely nothing that either man could want that wasn't readily available to them. But Mark did want something that he wasn't going to find by staring into that refrigerator.

He wanted Michelle. He was hungry for her, his desire so intense that he felt as if he were starving. Hunger pains didn't compare to the yearning he felt, wishing she were with him, in his arms, wanting him as much as he wanted her. Mark slammed the appliance door closed. Climbing back up the stairs, he crawled beneath his covers and wished for sleep, excited for tomorrow and the chance to spend more time with Michelle.

Chapter 13

Michelle found another bouquet of flowers with an anonymous card on her doorstep as she made her way out of her apartment door the next morning. Headed to work, she'd almost tripped over the delightful arrangement, surprised to find flowers waiting for her again.

It was a simple arrangement of white orchids with a single red rose adorning the center. She'd almost forgotten about the others, having been distracted when Mark had arrived at her door. The man had made light of them and although Michelle had found herself wishing that the bouquet had been from him, she wasn't quite so sure.

Mark hadn't reacted like a man who'd sent her flowers. He'd seemed as curious about them as she had been and now there was another beautiful arrangement.

With love from your secret admirer. Michelle read the card over again, almost believing that if she read it enough the cloak-and-dagger information wouldn't be classified anymore. She couldn't begin to figure out who the flowers were from, and there wasn't one identifying marker that might lead her to the answer.

Moving the flowers to the counter to sit with the others, Michelle locked her front door and headed for the track. Mark had promised to meet her for doughnuts and coffee and Michelle couldn't wait to start her day with the warmth of his brilliant smile.

As she slid into the driver's seat of her car she couldn't stop thinking about their time together. She was still in awe of the words she'd spoken, the emotions she was feeling exposed for the man to see. For a brief moment she'd been petrified that he'd be ready to run as far from her as he could get but the man had simply smiled, kissing every ounce of her fear from her.

Love. She'd told him she loved him. She'd not even been aware of the thought until it had spilled out of her mouth and then she had to face what she'd been most afraid of. She was in love with Mark Stallion. She'd fallen head over heels in love the very first time she'd laid eyes on him. Miami had served to solidify that Michelle wanted a man just like Mark to spend the rest of her life with. The man excited her. He made her feel special and the more time they spent in each other's company, the more time Michelle wanted to spend with him.

She and the man shared much in common. They had many of the same dreams and not one of them had anything to do with status or wealth. They were kindred spirits, seeking the same thrills and Michelle liked that what he imagined for his future easily rivaled the goals and dreams she had for herself.

She couldn't keep herself from wondering whether or not

Mark might be thinking about her right then the way she was thinking of him, but intuition told her she didn't need to worry. There was a connection between them that was undeniable. It had happened quickly and was building in intensity. The wealth of it was like nothing Michelle had ever known in her lifetime.

Michelle could feel herself smiling widely, a full grin highlighting her beauty. Mark Stallion had somehow managed to tame her, moving her to fathom a life with him at her side. Michelle couldn't help but wish that she had moved him as deeply, imagining that if a stallion like Mark could be tamed by any woman, then Michelle was the woman who could do just that.

Mark was waiting in the garage bay for her, peering beneath the hood of a car when she arrived at the track. His face warmed visibly at the sight of her as she moved in his direction to greet him.

Leaning forward to kiss her lips, he tossed her a quick wink as he pulled away. "Good morning, beautiful."

Michelle smiled back, a shy, sweet bend to her mouth. "Good morning."

The mechanic who'd been standing with Mark nodded his greetings then excused himself as he moved back to the vehicle he'd been working on earlier.

"So," Michelle asked, "what are you working on?"

"We need to get this one on a lift. The timing belt's gone."

"She's clicking badly, huh?"

Mark nodded. "It definitely isn't running smooth."

"It's a good thing you caught it before the engine blew. That would not have been pretty."

Mark moved to wrap his arms around her. "I actually didn't catch it. Mack told me you did, last week. He just did me a favor and passed on the information."

Michelle laughed. "I actually would have. He beat me to it."

"I just bet you would have," Mark said, laughing with her. The man kissed her again, allowing his mouth to linger atop hers until they were both dizzy.

Michelle fought to catch her breath, glancing quickly around to see if any of the others had been watching.

Mark chuckled. "I promise you, no one saw," he said warmly.

Michelle brushed a stray hair out of her eyes. "I wasn't worried," she answered, her tone hardly convincing.

Mark laughed. "Like heck you weren't."

Michelle skewed her face at him. "Well, what are people going to think if they see the two of us making out in the garage?"

"They're going to say that I'm a very lucky man, that's what they're going to say."

Michelle smiled. "Well, I don't want…"

Before she could finish her statement, there was a rustle of noise coming from the stadium doors on the other side of the large space. Both Mark and Michelle looked over to see what was going on. Mark's curious expression welcomed the two blue-suited men approaching where they stood. Michelle's face fell, annoyance pulling at her features.

She immediately recognized both of the officers from their previous conversation the afternoon before. The two men were investigating the numerous accidents that had happened since Michelle had signed on to work for Rockman and his crew. Michelle knew from the look the two were giving her that neither meant her any good.

"Ms. Coleman."

She nodded her head. "Officer Daniels, isn't it?"

The towheaded man with his spiky blond haircut bobbed his head up and down against his lean neck, flashing them both a quick look at his badge. "It's detective. Detective

Daniels," the man said with a hint of attitude in his voice. "We need you to come down to the station with us to answer some more questions."

"What's going on?" Mark asked, an air of formality rising in his own tone.

The two badges gave him a quick glance. "Who are you?" the other officer, a tall Latino with piercing blue-black eyes and an olive complexion queried.

Michelle could feel Mark bristle ever so slightly as he answered. "Mark Stallion. Now what's the problem, Detective?"

Recognition appeared in the officer's intense gaze. "We have an open investigation into the near fatal accidents of Mr. Boone and Mr. Foster. We're hoping Ms. Coleman can help us with some of the fuzzier details."

Mark tossed a quick glance in Michelle's direction. The color had drained from her face and, although she might have appeared calm and collected to someone who didn't know her well, he could tell she was anything but calm.

"Is Ms. Coleman being taken into custody?" Mark asked.

The two men glanced briefly at each other. "It's important Ms. Coleman come with us to talk but no, sir, she is not being taken into custody."

"Not yet," the other man added.

Michelle felt herself leaning toward Mark, wishing she could attach herself to his side and hold on. She didn't like where this was going and she was suddenly scared.

As if he could sense her distress, Mark eased a large hand around her waist, his palm resting protectively against the small of her back. "Ms. Coleman will be glad to answer any questions you have, Detective. But she won't be answering anything without legal counsel present." He checked the watch on his wrist before he continued. "Ms.

Coleman and her attorney will gladly meet you at the station in two hours."

The Latino man opened his mouth to speak, but the look his partner gave him cut his words off before he could ease them past his lips.

Mark seemed to stand two feet taller, his broad chest pushed forward, his shoulders tight, as if he were challenging either of them to say different.

Detective Daniels nodded his assent. "Thank you. Two hours then," he said, his displeasure evident.

As the two men walked back in the direction they'd come from, both tossing them looks of pure venom over their shoulders, Michelle began to shake, her knees threatening to give out beneath her.

"What's going on, Mitch?" Mark asked, turning to stand in front of her. "What do you have to do with any of this?"

"Nothing, but they seem to think I had something to do with all the accidents that have been happening around the tracks."

A look of surprise swept across Mark's face. "Why would they think…?" he started, not needing to finish the question.

Michelle shrugged. "I really don't know but everyone seems to believe I may have been responsible."

Mark inhaled, a deep breath filling his lungs with air. He exhaled a ragged breath then reached for the cell phone clipped to the waistband of his denim jeans.

"Who are you calling?" Michelle asked, eyeing him curiously.

"My legal team. We need to get them up to speed and we only have two hours to do it in," he answered.

Not knowing how to respond, Michelle said nothing. It had finally hit home that this wasn't going to go away quietly. She hadn't imagined she'd need any help clearing her name but now here Mark was, commandeering a legal team to come to her defense. She suddenly felt sick, bile threatening to rise out of the pit of her stomach.

Pressing her hand to his chest, Michelle closed her eyes and took two deep breaths. As Mark issued orders, she pointed in the direction of the restrooms and rushed toward the entrance. Just as the ladies' room door closed firmly behind her, the warm flow of saline came spilling out of her eyes.

The knock on Michelle's front door rumbled loudly through the enclosed space. As she stood staring out the living room window she was caught completely off guard. She wasn't expecting company, couldn't imagine who would be stopping by uninvited, and if the truth were told she was clearly not in the mood.

The couple standing on the other side of her entrance greeted her cheerily as she pulled the door open, looking from one unfamiliar face to the other. Michelle could barely muster the semblance of a smile as she greeted them warily.

"Ms. Coleman?" The man, tall and thin with eyes like green glass and a head of Lucille Ball curls smiled her name.

"May I help you?" Michelle answered.

The man extended a business card in her direction. "We're here from Dream Meals. My name's Bryan and this is my assistant, Paula. We're here to prepare dinner for you this evening." The woman named Paula waved a quick hand in Michelle's direction.

Taking the card, Michelle read it quickly. *Dream Meals— where wonderful meals start in your home!* "I'm sorry," Michelle said, "but I didn't order anything from you."

Bryan smiled. "No, ma'am, you didn't. But this may explain more," he finished, passing her a sealed envelope.

Taking the mailer, Michelle slid her thumb along the sealed flap and pulled out the neatly printed card inside. The hand-writing was becoming quite familiar. *Bon Appétit! With love from your Secret Admirer.*

Michelle looked from the card to the duo in front of her.

"You'll hardly know we're here," Paula said. "Just point us toward your kitchen and we'll have your meal ready in no time."

"Can you at least tell me who ordered you?" Michelle questioned, reluctance still pulling at her.

The man smiled. "I'm sorry but we don't know. Orders are placed through our central office. We only cook. But please, call the eight-hundred office number on our card to confirm that we are who we say we are. We want you to be comfort-able with us being in your home. We'll wait right here for you."

Michelle closed the door between them, twisting the business card anxiously through her fingers. They seemed to be legitimate with the bags of groceries they carried in their arms and the badges that identified them both, but she knew it was always better to be safe than sorry later on down the road. Dialing information, Michelle retrieved a local tele-phone number for the business and dialed. Minutes later, the store's owner confirmed the order and his employees, but couldn't tell her a thing about her benefactor. She moved back to her front entrance and pulled the door back open.

"Can we please come in and get started?" Paula queried.

Michelle paused for a brief moment, still baffled by who could be doing all of this. As she finally stepped back, opening the door to allow them to enter, she just knew Mark had to be behind all of this. Who else would go to such lengths to get her attention?

She pointed toward her kitchen and watched as the team of professional cooks quickly made themselves comfortable.

Before long pots and pans were simmering nicely, food and spices being blended beautifully together. Michelle moved back into her living room and sat down.

As she reached for her telephone she was briefly interrupted. "Ms. Coleman. Would you like a glass of wine?" Bryan was asking, extending a silver tray with a crystal wineglass in her direction.

"Thank you. It's been a rough day," Michelle answered, taking the drink being offered.

"That's why we're here, ma'am," the man said, filling her glass from a bottle of cabernet sauvignon. "You just sit back and relax and we'll have a nice meal ready for you in no time."

Michelle nodded, taking a sip of her wine as Bryan moved back to the kitchen, the decadent aromas steadily rising throughout the space. Savoring her drink, Michelle allowed herself to slowly relax. Remembering her telephone call, Michelle pulled the receiver into her hand and dialed.

Three rings later Mark answered. "Hello?"

"Hi, it's me."

Michelle could feel him smiling into the receiver. "Hi, yourself. How are you?"

"I just called to say thank you."

"Thank you? For what?"

"My dinner surprise."

Mark laughed. "I think the surprise is on me. I don't know what you're talking about."

"Dream Meals?"

"Okay. And they are…?"

"You didn't hire a private chef to come cook dinner for me? *Bon appétit, your secret admirer?*" Michelle asked, quoting from the card.

Mark chuckled. "Sorry, darling, but it's not me. Someone sent you dinner?"

Michelle nodded into the receiver. "My own private, in-home, gourmet restaurant."

"I really need to find out who this secret admirer is. This guy's trying to give me a run for my money," Mark said teasingly.

There was an awkward pause as Michelle drifted off in thought. Who was sending her these gifts, she wondered, not having a clue who'd be interested in playing these games with her.

"Mitch? You still there?"

Mark's seductive tone pulled her back to the moment. Michelle shook the clouds from her head. "Yes, I'm sorry. I was just…"

"Trying to decide if you're going to give me a hint about my competition or not?"

She laughed, rolling her eyes skyward. "Trying to figure out who your competition might be."

"So you admit I've got competition?"

Michelle laughed again. "Let's change the subject. What are you doing for dinner?"

This time Mark laughed. "I really hope I'm doing something that's going to annoy the heck out of your secret admirer."

"So how soon do you think you can get here?" Michelle queried.

Mark grinned on the other end. "I'm on my way."

Disconnecting the call, Mark gestured for his brother's attention. Matthew was circling the paddock on the back of a new stallion he'd recently acquired. The two had been at the ranch, down in the stables, ever since Mark had returned from the police station with Michelle.

He thought about the tense encounter they'd had with Dallas's finest. Even the swift meeting he'd had with the district attorney, a good friend of the family's, hadn't left him with any warm and fuzzy feelings.

There was something about the whole mess that wasn't adding up and Mark didn't know how to begin to make all the pieces fit. The dynamic duo had interrogated Michelle for over an hour, repeating the same questions and getting the same answers again and again.

The woman had been adamant about her innocence, steadily denying that she'd had anything to do with any of the mess they were accusing her of. But everything seemed to point in Michelle's direction, the woman having had access and motive if anyone believed what the police wanted everyone to believe. The two men who'd been injured had all worked with or for her father. Michelle had been heard blaming them for one thing or another shortly after her father's death. Michelle had been seen in the garage with one driver's vehicle just before it had exploded. She'd been in the work bay in the vicinity of the other victim's ride offering him advice just before his accident. It all made sense if one were inclined to connect the many dots local enforcement had laid out for them to connect. And now, Mark wasn't quite sure what he was supposed to believe.

During the ride to the ranch from the police station, Matthew had picked up on his confusion, pulling at the doubt that seemed to have risen between him and Michelle. The two had talked for some time before Mark found himself able to relax and hope for the best. Matthew had encouraged him to trust his instincts about her, to hold steadfast to what he was feeling for Michelle. And despite the skepticism that continued to linger in his thoughts, Mark was anxious to get back to her side and spend some time with her.

Matthew and the horse lumbered up beside him, the duo coming to a halt at the fence Mark sat atop. "Hey, what's up?"

"I'm heading out. Michelle called and invited me to dinner."

His brother nodded. "That's good. It'll give you two some time to talk about what's going on. You might get some better perspective about the whole thing. Maybe she'll share something with you she didn't tell the police."

"Maybe," Mark said, not totally convinced that he wanted to know more.

Matthew could see the concern that painted his expression. He could only begin to imagine what his brother might have been thinking about the woman who seemed to have laid claim to his heart. He offered some encouragement.

"I'm sure everything is going to be just fine," Matthew said, meeting his brother's gaze.

Mark smiled, swinging his legs back over the fence. Dropping down to the ground, he gave Matthew a quick wink. "Take it easy, big brother," he said, trying not to let his mood show in his voice. "And thanks for listening."

With a quick wave of his hand, Matthew and his horse galloped off in the opposite direction. Behind them, Mark stood staring off into space, wondering if he really knew anything at all about the woman he'd fallen in love with.

Chapter 14

Her dining room table had actually been set with the never used dishes that filled the glass curio cabinet in her dining room. Michelle didn't entertain often and past gatherings had only required paper plates and plastic utensils. As she admired the presentation, Michelle made a mental note to make sure she did this again, enjoying the not-so-casual flair in her formal living space.

Mark pulled out her chair, gesturing for her to take a seat.

"Thank you," Michelle chimed sweetly.

"No, thank you," Mark responded, pulling out his own chair and taking a seat. "Thank you for sharing your gift with me."

Michelle smiled. "If only I knew who my gift was from."

"That still has you baffled, huh?"

She gave him a curious stare. "Something you'd like to admit to, Mr. Stallion?"

Mark shook his head and laughed. It was deep rumble that

erupted from deep in his midsection. Michelle found the wealth of it to be contagious and soon she was laughing heartily with him.

Wiping a tear from his eye, Mark gasped, inhaling deeply to catch his breath. When he could finally speak again he grinned widely. "Sorry, kiddo. Although I would like to, I can't take the credit for this or the flowers."

Michelle wiped at her own eyes. "If you say so—"

Mark stalled her comment. "Seriously, Mitch, this isn't my doing, baby. But I'm glad that the brother who is doing this hasn't showed himself yet."

"And why is that?"

"Because he'd be intruding on my time with you and I can't have that. I'm trying to win your heart. I can't have some other guy messing that up."

"Why does that sound like some macho, male ego, mess?"

Mark chuckled. "Because it is. I can't let some other guy outshine me now," Mark exclaimed.

"Aren't you the least bit curious who my admirer might be?" Michelle asked curiously.

Mark shrugged. "Do you want me to be?"

Michelle paused, not quite sure how to take the man's attitude. There wasn't a hint of jealousy or annoyance at the thought of another man being interested in her. Mark seemed to read her mind as he reached for her hand, pressing his palm against the back of her closed fist.

"Mitch, I know how I feel about you and I know how you feel about me. I don't need to be jealous or upset because some other guy is trying to get your attention. If I can't trust that you and I truly have something between us then we don't need to be doing this. I trust what I feel and I'm trusting what I think you feel, too."

Before Michelle could respond, Paula appeared with a large tray of food, Bryan following closely on her heels. The man was still grinning like a Cheshire cat, the wide smile filling his narrow face.

"Thank you for making enough for two," Michelle said

They both smiled. "It wasn't a problem at all," Bryan said.

After the meal was served, Bryan and Paula dismissed themselves, only leaving Michelle with the plates on the table to clear away. She was impressed when Mark tipped the two handsomely, claiming to be paying for his share of the meal.

Plates of Caesar salad with homemade croutons and an entrée of penne pasta tossed with chicken and vegetables in a decadent cream sauce graced the table. Michelle couldn't even begin to imagine having done something like that herself. Throughout the meal, conversation flowed easily between the two, both enjoying the camaraderie. They were thrilled at the little things they were discovering about each other, enjoying what felt like the perfect ending to a not-so-perfect day.

Dinner was followed by dessert, a chocolate torte that melted like warm butter in their mouths and, without having asked, a pot of freshly brewed coffee was waiting to finish off the meal. The food was too good and when Michelle was just a bite away from being overstuffed, she pushed her plate away from her, moving to lean back against her chair.

"That was delicious!" she exclaimed, wiping at her mouth with a cloth napkin.

Mark followed suit. "Yes, it was. I could definitely do this again," he said, smiling warmly.

Michelle nodded in agreement as she reached for his plate. Mark stalled her, lifting her dish and his own from the table.

"I think I can handle this," he said firmly. "At least let me finish the dishes."

The woman giggled. "I was just going to put them in the dishwasher."

"Like I said, I can handle that," Mark chuckled. "Now, the dishwasher is that thing that sits under the counter by the sink, right?" he said teasingly.

Michelle laughed out loud. "Yes, it is."

Mark winked and disappeared into the kitchen, leaving her alone for a brief moment. When he returned, Michelle had moved from the dining room into the living room, settling herself comfortably down on the sofa. As he stepped into the room she patted the empty seat beside her, beckoning him to sit down.

"Thank you," Michelle offered, breaking the silence that had settled in the space. "I really didn't get a chance to tell you earlier how much I appreciate what you did for me today at the police station."

"I would never let you go through something like that by yourself, Mitch. Especially if there is something I can do to help."

"Well, it really meant a lot to me."

"Well, you're very welcome," Mark said, leaning to kiss her lips. He lingered in the moment, allowing his lips to brush easily over hers.

Michelle felt her nipples stiffen. A pleasing warm sensation spiraled through her lower belly down into her sweet spot. As Mark pulled away, she found herself breathless, her gaze locked with his.

"That was very nice," she said, her voice coming huskily.

"It was," Mark agreed, moving to wrap his arms around her shoulder.

Michelle allowed herself to settle down against the man, her head resting against his shoulder.

Silence resurfaced between them, the duo falling into the

warmth of quiet that had dropped down around them. Thoughtful, they sat reflecting on their day and each other. Without warning, a questioning glaze seemed to cross Mark's expression and Michelle could sense a sudden change in his mood.

"What's the matter, Mark?" she asked, peering up into his face.

The man paused, searching for the right words to ask what had been on his mind since their earlier meeting. "Mitch, did you have anything at all to do with what happened. I mean...I'd understand if it was an accident. I'm sure you..."

He could feel her bristle, denial spinning out of her eyes. "You don't believe me."

"No, Mitch, it's not that..."

"Then what is it? If you believed me you wouldn't have to ask if I'd done anything."

"It could have just been accidental. Maybe you forgot to tighten up a clamp or..."

Michelle sprang up out of her seat, moving to the other side of the room, her arms hugging her torso. "I didn't do anything wrong and I resent you thinking that I could possibly—"

Mark rose from his seat, moving to her side as he interrupted her. "I'm sorry, Mitch. I didn't mean to upset you. I just..."

Michelle stood stiffly in his arms, not bothering to reach her own arms around him. Her perfect evening had suddenly soured and now she just wanted him to leave her home. "I think it's time for you to leave," she said coolly.

Mark closed his eyes tightly, and then opened them to stare down at her. "I didn't mean to upset you, Mitch," he said, contrition painting his expression.

"Well, you have and now I want you to get out of my home." Pushing him away from her, she crossed her arms over her chest.

Mark stood like stone in the center of the room, having not a clue what to say or do to make amends for the insult. Everything about Michelle's body language told him she wasn't going to let this go as quickly as he had hoped. But he'd had doubts and questions and Michelle was the only one he could get the answers from. He made the effort to explain that to her. "No," he said, his position resolute. "I'm not going anywhere until we make things right between us."

Michelle sighed in frustration. But her shoulders still felt heavy, the burden of the accusations being more than she had ever imagined them to be. She had trusted Mark. She'd believed that he had trusted her. She felt she didn't know what to believe anymore. The two stood staring intensely at each other.

"I just didn't know what was true and what wasn't true," Mark was saying. He gripped her by the shoulder, fighting for her attention. "I know how much your father's death affected you, Mitch. I didn't know if you still blamed his old crew or his competitors for what happened or not. You might have thought you were avenging his death. I just didn't know."

Michelle shook her head. "No, you didn't. But I thought you'd gotten to know me well enough to know that I would never hurt another person like that. Those men could have been killed. Their families could be missing them the way I miss my dad right now. I can't believe you'd actually think I'd do that to someone else's child. Now get out of my home."

The icy stare she gave him sent a chill straight down Mark's spine. He couldn't believe that their wonderful evening had turned on a dime to a night of sheer disaster. This wasn't what he'd wanted. And he didn't have a clue how to make it all better again.

Before he could say anything else, Michelle stomped to the

front door, pulling it open. With one hand on her hip and the other clamped around the doorknob, she gestured for him to get out. Mark tried to plead his case.

"Mitch, baby, please. Let's just talk…"

Michelle cut him off, her tone biting. "I'm not going to ask you again to get out of my home. The next time I'm not going to be so polite," she said through clenched teeth.

Recognizing that there was nothing he could do to shift her mood, Mark crossed the room and made his exit. Behind him the door slammed harshly, the rage of it vibrating through the evening air.

Rockman could barely contain his grin when Michelle entered his office space. The woman looked around, frustration masking her features. Every time she stepped foot into the space Michelle felt like she'd stepped back into a time warp. Everything was gold and ornate, from the velvet, floor-to-ceiling drapes, the two-toned shag carpeting and the brocade furniture. Michelle imagined the space was once considered stylish with its overdone and outlandish flair, but she wanted to tell her employer that much less would be so much more now. She fought back the urge to chuckle, bemusement painting her expression.

Rockman rushed from behind his desk to greet her. "Mitch! How are you doing, honey?" he asked, feigning concern.

Michelle smiled warmly. "Fine, thank you, Uncle Greg. How are you, sir?"

The man nodded, his bulbous head waving on the end of his neck like a bubble-headed doll gone awry. "Have a seat, dear. Make yourself comfortable," he intoned, guiding her by the elbow to the lavish paisley-printed love seat. "Take a load off."

Michelle's smile still pulled at her mouth, her facial

muscles frozen politely. "Your secretary said you needed to see me, sir?"

Rockman's head continue to bobble. "This nasty business with the authorities is making more work for us business owners than is necessary. I wanted to see how you're doing, dear."

Michelle twisted her hands nervously in her lap. "I'm well, Uncle Greg, thank you. I'm sorry that this is happening though."

"Well, I hope you know that we fully support you. No one here at Rockman would ever think you'd do anything out of line."

"Thank you, Uncle Greg. That means a lot to me."

Rockman rested a chubby palm against Michelle's knee, his clammy flesh connecting with her leather bike pants. "Mitch, we're all family here. You know how close your daddy and I were. He'd want me to make sure you were well taken care of."

A tear rose to Michelle's eye and she swiped it away with the back of her hand. "Thank you, sir. I appreciate that."

Rockman patted her leg, then jumped to his feet. "Now, you remember, if there's anything you want to talk to me about, my door is always open to you. I'm sure all this mess will go away soon. I'm sure it's just some bitter rivalry. Folks don't like it when you're on top, Mitch, and you've got us on top. The competition is liable to do anything to knock us down. I for one wouldn't put it past that Stallion team to be responsible for all this mess!" he exclaimed, eyeing Michelle carefully for a reaction.

Michelle bristled, her muscles tensing. She didn't bother to respond, her own gaze meeting Rockman's evenly.

"You and Stallion seem pretty close, Mitch. You sure you can trust him?"

"Mr. Stallion seems to be an upstanding man. I doubt highly that he could be behind any of this," she finally said, her tone wavering with a hint of anger.

"I'm sure. I'm sure," Rockman said halfheartedly. "But you never know. Money can buy him all kinds of loyalty. I hear it said that a few of his friends are a little unscrupulous."

Michelle rose to her feet. "I've never heard that," she said. "Is there anything else you need to speak with me about, Uncle Greg?"

The man shrugged his wide shoulders. "No, Mitch. Like I said, I just wanted to check in and let you know I'm here if you need me."

Michelle moved toward the office door. "Thank you," she said, her hand rotating the doorknob.

Rockman grinned. "Your daddy was my friend, Mitch. I wouldn't disappoint him or you."

Not bothering to respond, Michelle exited the room. Rockman stared after her, the expression on his face dropping drastically the minute he was out of her sight. This was going to have to come to a head sooner than later. Final competitions would soon be starting and there was much that needed to be done to insure his team's success. Stallion and his team were running too close on his heels, just seconds away from pulling the title out of his best racer's hands and Rockman wasn't going to have that. He needed to move and move quick before all his best work was for naught. He was beginning to wonder what he was paying for because clearly what he needed accomplished wasn't happening fast enough.

As the door slammed closed behind Michelle's departure, Rockman pulled his cell phone into his hands and dialed. Minutes later Detective Daniels answered the other line.

Simon threw his hands up in the air in exasperation. A week had passed since Michelle had thrown Mark out of her home and here she was still slamming car parts and tools around, refusing to open up and tell him who or what had her so angry. He had just about had enough when she came storming back into the office, finally ready to speak.

"I don't know what to do," she exclaimed, tears welling in her eyes as she dropped into one of the wooden seats behind the counter. Her gaze skated across Simon's face, searching for an answer. "Why is this happening to me?"

"What's going on, Mitch? This isn't like you. This isn't like you at all."

Michelle sighed deeply. "He doesn't believe me."

"Who, baby? Who doesn't believe you about what?"

"Mark. He's not sure if I had something to do with the accidents at the track or not."

Simon sighed. "So, you heard all that talk that's been going around?"

Michelle cut her gaze in her uncle's direction. "How long have you known?"

"Some of the boys came and told me what was going around a few days back."

Michelle opened her mouth to speak but Simon stalled her, holding his hand out in front of him. "Before you say it, I didn't tell you because I didn't think there was anything to tell. You know how these fools can be sometimes. I didn't think anything else would come of it once I let them all know that kind of talk wasn't appreciated."

Michelle heaved a deep sigh. "Well, something has come of it. The police are investigating and I'm their number-one suspect," she said, relating the events from her visit down at the station and Mark affording her the best legal help his money could buy. Then she told him what Rockman had implied about Mark.

"That's ridiculous," Simon said. "Don't nobody wit' no

good sense think you or that boy could have done something like that."

"Mark does. He asked me if I'd done it."

Simon rolled his eyes. "I'm sure that boy doesn't believe you had anything to do with none of this. Not that he doesn't have any good sense. He was probably just—"

"Just what? Just trying to make sure? He doubted me, Uncle Simon. I thought he knew me better than that."

The old man nodded slowly. "Would you have felt better if he hadn't asked you? If he'd had questions and didn't tell you?"

"No, of course not, but…"

"But he asks you and now you're mad?"

"I'm angry that he didn't trust me."

"You two are just getting to know each other good. He'd have been a fool if he didn't ask."

"Are you defending him?"

"I'm just looking at it from his point of view. Put yourself in his place. What would you have done if the shoe was on the other foot?"

Michelle sat staring at Simon, imagining what she would have done if Mark had been the one they'd been accusing. She sighed again. The more she thought about it, the more she realized that she couldn't fault him. The evidence was too coincidental. If she didn't know any better she might have been questioning her own self. Common sense told her not to take his reservations personally, but her heart still stung from the infraction. She knew there was nothing personal about him wanting to be sure of what he was getting himself into. Michelle would have done the same, asking the same questions of him had she been in his shoes.

She dropped her head into her hands, swiping at a tear that had fallen against her cheek. "So, what do I do now?" she asked, not bothering to look back up at her uncle. "How do I fix this?"

"Well, answer me this first. Do you think there's anything to what Rockman said? Is it possible that Mark did have something to do with this mess?"

Michelle shook her head vehemently. "Of course not. Mark's not like that."

Simon nodded. "But you thought about it after Rockman said it, didn't you? Couldn't help but maybe wonder if there might be something to it, right?"

Michelle shrugged. "Maybe I did. But I know him. He's a good man."

"Maybe you do and then again, maybe you don't. I'm sure though that if there were enough fingers pointing in his direction you'd be willing to ask him because you care about him the way you do."

A pause filled the space between them, swelling full as Michelle mulled over all that the old man had said. She suddenly felt herself agreeing, annoyed that her uncle's wisdom seemed to be outshining her own.

Simon wrapped his arms around her torso, hugging her tightly. "Let that boy help you, Mitch. Don't let that pride of yours get in your way."

Michelle leaned back in her seat, looking as if the weight of the world was resting atop her shoulders. "And what if I do let him help. Then what?"

"Then we figure out together what's going on. We know you didn't do it and that means we need to figure out who did."

Michelle nodded, rising from her seat. "If I drank, Uncle Simon, I'd drink right now."

Simon chuckled. "Go tear apart an engine instead. Then stop being mad at the boy and give him a call. Okay?"

"Okay," Michelle whispered softly as she headed back in the direction of the garage.

Simon called after her. "Mitch?"

"Yes, sir?"

"We're going to figure this out, baby. I promise."

Michelle smiled, her mouth lifting ever so slightly. "I know we will, Uncle Simon. And I love you, too."

Watching her walk away, Simon's stare suddenly turned serious. Whatever was happening was bad. Almost as bad as when Michelle's father had been killed. Fixing this wasn't going to be easy. If Michelle didn't call that Stallion fellow, Simon knew he would. He knew they would need all the help they could get to save Michelle from whoever was trying to do her harm.

"Numb nuts! What were you thinking?" Vanessa exclaimed.

Mark shrugged. "I don't know what I was thinking, Vanessa."

His best friend crossed her arms over her chest as she dropped down onto the sofa beside the man. "Do you really think Mitch had something to do with all those accidents? I mean really, do you actually believe that is the kind of woman you've fallen in love with?"

"Who said I was in love?"

Vanessa laughed. "Are you denying it?"

"I'm not saying anything about it at all."

"Because you know you're in love with Mitch," Vanessa giggled.

Mark didn't bother to respond, pretending to leaf through the pages of a cycling magazine.

Vanessa sat watching him, his distress obvious in the lines that creased his forehead. "Okay," she said, finally breaking the silence. "When are you going to call and beg for forgiveness? Because you need to do it soon."

"Why should I—" Mark started.

Vanessa cut him off. "Because you hurt her feelings! Duh! Don't you know women don't like it when they think their men don't believe in them?"

"How would you know?" Mark said, his tone sarcastic. "It's not like you've ever dated a man."

Vanessa shot him a look that told him to tread cautiously. "I know enough to know when a man has done something incredibly stupid. And what you did was dumb. You love her and she loves you. You know you didn't need to question her like that."

"I know," he said with resignation. "The thought just crossed my mind and before I could think it through I opened my mouth and stuck in my foot. She'll probably never speak to me again."

"She will but you need to call her."

Mark suddenly stood up. "I need to go stand on her doorstep and beg is what I need to do."

Vanessa grinned. "Begging is good. Women like begging."

Mark smiled back. "How would you know?" he asked teasingly.

"I've had to beg a woman or two back in the day."

"I thought you had the female market on point? What could you possibly have done wrong?"

Vanessa laughed. "You men don't have the exclusivity on dumb mistakes," she said. "Women make their fair share as well."

Mark chuckled. "I know that's right," he said, waving as he headed out the door. "I know that's right!"

Chapter 15

It was well past midnight when Michelle finally found her way home. She'd been thinking about Mark most of the day, and thoughts of him still lingered. She'd been half tempted to seek out his home, but had talked herself out of it as she'd driven past the pricey gated community. Talking herself out of things had always kept her out of trouble. Had she talked herself out of going out with Mark that first time she probably wouldn't be in this mess with him right now, she thought to herself, making her way to her front door.

She entered the complex through the landscaped courtyard and up the stairs to her front door. Mark sat in front of her entrance, his long legs extended over the stoop, his head and back resting against the door frame. The man was sound asleep, dozing comfortably as Michelle made her way to his side.

Smiling down at him, Michelle couldn't help but be

amused. Mark was snoring softly, a line of drool puddled at the corner of his lips as he sat with his head back and his mouth open. Michelle could only begin to imagine what he'd been thinking to have been waiting there for her. She shook him gently, careful not to scare him out of his sleep.

"Mark. Sweetheart. Wake up," Michelle said, leaning to press her lips to his forehead. "Baby, you can't sleep out here," she said.

Mark jumped slightly, his eyes opening wide as looked about anxiously. Focus came slowly as he remembered where he was and what he was doing there. "Michelle. Where were you? I was waiting for you."

Michelle smiled sweetly. "I'm sorry. I was at the garage. Are you all right?"

Mark nodded, stretching the last remnants of sleep from his muscles. "I'm stiff. It's not too comfortable out here."

Michelle extended a hand to help him to his feet. "I don't imagine it is. Why don't you come on inside," she said as she pushed her key into the lock and opened the door.

Mark followed behind her, securing the entry after they made their way inside. As Michelle turned to face him, his apology spilled into the room. "Baby girl, I am so sorry. I should never have doubted you. Never. I know you'd never hurt anyone. I was stupid for asking you the way I did. Lord knows I would never do anything to hurt you. Please believe me." He took a step closer to her, moving to loop his arms around her torso. "I'm so sorry, Mitch. Will you forgive me?"

Michelle allowed him to pull her close, holding her tightly in his arms. She leaned her head into his chest. It felt good in his arms, safe and secure and suddenly she couldn't remember what it was she'd been so angry about. All she knew was that she had missed him terribly and that no matter what happened from that point forward she would never let her anger, or his, get between them.

Something the man had said the last time they'd been together suddenly sprang into her thoughts. She took a step back, staring up at him. Mark eyed her questioningly.

"What?" he asked, unable to read her expression.

"You don't have anything to worry about," she said softly, reaching to hold his hand.

Mark shook his head. "I don't understand."

"You don't ever have to worry about my secret admirer," she said, a slight bend to her lips lifting her mouth into a faint smile. "You've already won my heart, Mark Stallion."

Mark smiled back. Stepping toward her, he closed the gap, reaching to lift her chin in the palm of his hand. Leaning in slowly, he stared into her eyes, refusing to break the connection that had him falling head over heels into the depths of her gaze. And then he kissed her, easing every ounce of that earlier tension away.

Michelle didn't know how long they'd stood in her foyer kissing. Her lips were swollen sweetly, Mark's mouth deliciously bruising her own. When he finally let her go, both of them coming up for some much needed air, she was dizzy with wanting, her entire body feeling as if it were about to combust.

"Stay the night," Michelle said, fighting to get the words past her lips. "Make love to me," she said, the request just a fraction away from being a command.

Mark reached for her hand. Michelle followed as he led her down the hall toward her bedroom, following the faint rays of moonlight that glistened through her windows. Inside Michelle's private space, Mark moved to the bathroom, opening the door and switching on the light. Michelle stood watching as he turned on the tub's faucet and began to run a bath of warm water.

Minutes later, Mark gestured for her to join him, extending his hand in her direction. As she came to stand before him, he slowly began to remove her clothes, undoing her buttons one by one and sliding the garments off her body. Michelle marveled at the soft touch of his fingers against her skin, his hands burning like fire against her flesh.

Without saying a word, Mark pointed toward the filled tub, a wry smile decorating his face. As Michelle stepped into the pool of rose-scented bubbles, a steady pounding began to throb between her legs. Standing above her, Mark began to take off his own clothes. The moment was surreal as he dropped his black dress slacks and white cotton shirt against the tiled floor. Michelle was in awe of him, every muscle firm and rigid as he stood like a black Adonis before her. Easing into the large garden tub behind her, Mark wrapped his body around hers, pulling Michelle back against his naked chest, a heavy erection pressing hard against her lower back. Electricity rippled back and forth between them.

He filled a cupped palm with water and slowly dribbled the warm flow up and over her body. It felt like liquid gold across the sensitive nipples that had blossomed full and hard beneath his ministrations. Michelle gasped at the stimulation as Mark twirled the hard candy flesh between his thumb and forefinger, his mouth trailing damp kisses against her neck. Falling into the moment, Michelle's thoughts were clouded as Mark whispered warm breath against her ear.

"You are so sweet, Mitch," he muttered softly, his tongue trailing a path along her neck and up to the line of her ear. As Michelle lifted her head slightly into the gesture Mark eased his tongue into the cavity. Michelle could hear herself moan, Mark's name teasing the tip of her own tongue.

Reaching for one of the bathing puffs that sat on the edge of the porcelain pool, Mark applied a liberal amount of floral-scented body wash to the puff's surface. With slow, easy strokes he began to caress her shoulders, scrubbing lightly at her arms and down her back. Soon a considerable lather bubbled over her skin and down her backside. Easing his hands across her front, lather flowed over her breasts, trailing down to her belly button and back into the water that surrounded them. Mark's fingers lightly brushed at the crevice between her legs, but the man restrained himself from allowing his fingers to slip between her thighs.

Michelle felt the warmth of Mark's breath brushing against her ear as he whispered her name. All rational thought seemed to have left her as a cramping sensation between her legs momentarily took her breath away. The delicate hairs at the back of her neck stood at attention. Behind her, Mark was smiling, savoring the knowledge of just how much more intense the pleasure they would share would be.

The two lingered in the warmth of the water until every muscle had relaxed into jelly, both feeling content as they slowly massaged and stroked every ounce of stress away. As the water began to cool, Michelle lifted herself from the bath, reaching for one of the large bath towels folded against the countertop. Mark followed behind her, using his towel to brush the last remnants of water from the woman's skin.

Michelle closed her eyes tightly, enjoying the sensual pleasure that was ebbing beneath her flesh, the wealth of it ignited by the man's tenacious touch. Leading her back into the bedroom, Mark moved to light the row of scented candles atop her nightstand. As he did, Michelle reached for the Bose radio and turned on the melodic sounds of someone's jazz. The moment was captivating and for just a brief moment they stared at each other, a wealth of emotion like a raging tide between them.

Mark extended his arms, reaching for her, and as she lifted herself against the edge of the mattress, kneeling before him, the man couldn't help but acknowledge the sheer perfection of her beauty. Michelle was like no woman he'd ever known before, every ounce of his spirit dancing in sync with hers. He pressed a gentle kiss to her forehead, then jumped ever so slightly as Michelle trailed her tongue over one nipple and then another, moving down his chest until she was lapping hungrily at the hollow of his belly button. Energy surged with a force he'd never experienced before, the moment causing his knees to quiver, threatening to drop him straight to the floor. He inhaled swiftly, fighting to maintain some control.

Pressing his hands to her shoulders, Mark pushed her gently back against the mattress. As he smiled down at her, Michelle wanted nothing more than to wrap her arms around his body and pull him close to her. When she reached for him Mark shook his head no, determined to control the moment.

Kneeling at the foot of the bed, he dragged Michelle's hips toward him and lifted her smooth thighs onto his shoulders. Michelle gasped loudly, her body quivering in anticipation of his touch. "Oh, Mark," Michelle panted as the man nuzzled her love button with the tip of his tongue. "Oh, baby, please," she gasped, the palm of her hand reaching down to press against the back of his head.

Mark didn't need any encouragement. Spreading the woman's legs he claimed his prize. Michelle was throbbing, milky nectar blossoming from the flower that opened to his touch. His tongue was already testing and tasting the sweet nectar that spilled from the delicate folds of her secret treasure. The young woman's hips began to heave as his drew her into his mouth, capturing the sensitive nub and gently sucking at the treat.

She was sweet, a delicacy for him to savor and explore and as he did, thrusting his tongue as deep as he could into her, Michelle screamed his name as she slammed her thighs tight against his ears. Writhing with pleasure, Michelle couldn't imagine that she could take much more as an orgasm rocketed through her body. The explosion of pleasure was so intense that Michelle thought for sure that she would pass out and never recover.

What happened next was indescribable as Mark lifted his body above hers, sheathing himself quickly with a condom as he plunged himself against her. Matching his rhythm, Michelle thrust her body against his, savoring each and every stroke. Mark could barely breathe as he slid in and out of her, Michelle's body locked tightly around his own. The moment was heated, the two of them dripping with sweat. He felt himself buck wildly as Michelle sucked the flesh beneath his chin, her tongue flicking back and forth across his neck. Her kisses were sweet, each one burning hotly against his skin.

The mind-numbing pleasure was everywhere and nowhere at once. It was as if they had floated right out of their bodies, their connection no longer an earthly one. Mark pressed his face into her neck, tears spilling out of his eyes as he called her name over and over again and then he said what he'd been thinking all evening long, the words spilling out of his mouth as he spilled himself inside her.

"I love you, Michelle Coleman. I love you!"

And as he dropped his body heavily against hers, cradling himself tightly around her, Michelle answered him back. "I love you, too, Mark. With all my heart."

Chapter 16

The morning sun shone brightly, highlighting their naked bodies as they lay tangled in Michelle's sheets. A smile pulled at Michelle's mouth as she leaned up on one elbow to stare down at the man sleeping peacefully beside her, his broad back gleaming beneath the early daylight. She eyed him with appreciation, his buttocks like two large, firm cantaloupes pressed tightly together. Every inch of his body was thick, muscles taut beneath flesh that gleamed like polished marble.

Michelle imagined she could easily rest a full glass of champagne on the shelf of his behind and not worry about spilling a drop. She couldn't resist trailing her hand across the firm flesh, leaning to press her lips against his expansive back. The man was a picture-perfect specimen of maleness, and just hours earlier he'd professed his love. Michelle shook her head from side to side, in awe that for the first time her love life might actually be something she could be happy about.

Mark stirred ever so slightly and Michelle leaned down to cover his body with her own. She liked how it felt to have a man in her bed when she woke in the morning. She realized she could easily get use to such a phenomenon.

Mark stretched his body lengthwise, slowly opening his eyes and allowing his vision to adjust to the bright rays pouring in around him. Michelle was warm against him and he didn't want to move but so much lest she move away from him. It felt right to have her spooning against his back, her naked flesh heating his own. The woman pressed a kiss against the back of his neck, her tongue trailing across his skin. His morning erection surged full and hard as he pressed his pelvis tight against the mattress.

"Good morning," Michelle said softly. "Did you sleep well?"

Mark smiled, humming softly. "Hmm. Yes, I did. I slept very well. How about you?"

The woman nodded against his back. "I slept very well."

Mark rolled his body until he was facing her, his arms wrapping her close against him. "I vote that we stay right here for the whole day. What do you say?"

Michelle laughed. "I second that vote but you have a race to run this evening and I've got work to do before that happens."

"What happens if you don't go to work?"

"Your team might beat mine."

Mark laughed with her. "We're going to do that no matter what so you might as well stay and spend the morning in bed with me."

"So this is how you stall your competition? Get them all light-headed and giddy so they can't think straight?"

Mark nodded. "Is it working?"

The woman's joy was contagious, mirth spilling out into the room. "No," she said, pretending not to be affected by his charms.

Mark closed his eyes, a large hand pulling through the length of her hair. "Can't fault a guy for trying," he said softly.

Michelle lifted herself up, throwing her legs off the side of the bed. "I need a shower," she said softly, her hand still stroking his chest with light abandon.

Mark nodded, watching as she stood up on her feet. Turning to face him, she extended her hand toward his. "Would you like to join me?" Michelle asked sweetly, her invitation leaving little to the imagination.

Grinning boldly, Mark nodded, allowing her to pull him from beneath the bedsheets and lead him to the bathroom, their fingers entwined tightly together. Inside the bathroom, Mark stood like stone, staring with appreciation. Michelle was beauty personified, an exquisite delight for the eyes, and Mark felt himself growing warm with intense desire. A protrusion of rock-hard flesh pulled taut, a raging erection pressing obscenely in front of him. Mark resisted the urge to reach out and touch her, enthralled by the sheer sight of her standing naked before him.

Michelle's dazzling gaze never left his as her hands reached for him, fingers teasing as they skated slowly across his chest, edging down to his abdomen. She leaned to press her mouth to his skin, leaving a trail of warm wet kisses across his torso. Michelle gently stroked each muscled line of his bare body, her exploration inciting his own. The man's own expression was lustful and she couldn't remember the last time a man had stared so appreciatively. Moving toward the shower, Mark adjusted the spray of hot water. Behind him, Michelle pressed herself against his back, drawing light kisses over his broad shoulders.

The woman's touch was pure magic, Mark thought, closing his eyes to enjoy the sensations that suddenly flooded through him. The steam rising in the space added to the seductive ambiance. Michelle moved into the shower first, Mark stepping in eagerly behind her. As the spray of warm water rained down over them, Mark allowed himself to touch her for the first time.

His hands danced along her curvaceous frame, his fingers memorizing each and every dip and dimple. Her nipples hardened like rock candy between the thumb and index finger that had captured them. A low moan eased past her lips as Mark palmed her flesh, her nipples pressed against the palms of his large hands. The man's mouth was dancing against the line of her profile, over her chin to her neck and down to capture the breast that he'd been playing with so wantonly.

Michelle felt as if she were about to explode, heat raging from one end of her body to the other. Leaning back into the spray of water, she let it shower down over her head and face, pulling Mark beneath the water with her. As water rained down over them, Michelle folded herself into Mark's arms, pressing her nakedness against his, savoring every moment of skin kissing skin.

When their lips reunited, both of them melted one into the other. It was poetry in motion as tongues danced in perfect unison. Mark savored the sweetness of Michelle's mouth, moaning his pleasure against her lips. He slid his fingers into her hair as he kissed her harder, craving as much of her as she would allow him to have. His lips slid from her mouth along the edge of her jaw, up to her ear. He nibbled lightly at her earlobe before whispering in her ear, "You are the most amazing woman I've ever known and I want to taste every square inch of you over and over again."

Michelle could feel herself smile at the possibilities as Mark nuzzled a trail of kisses back to her neck. "Is that so," she purred, relishing the wicked sensation of his mouth against her skin, every nerve ending sensitive to his touch.

"That is if you'll allow me to," he said, tilting his face to meet her gaze. The glazed look she gave him was filled with passion.

Michelle nodded. "I guess I'm yours to do with what you want," she said, smiling sweetly in his direction. "Then, of course, I get to do you back," she finished as she boldly wrapped her hand around his penis. She squeezed him gently and Mark shuddered from the intense pleasure.

"Oh, baby," he whispered, kissing her one more time as they both moved beneath the flow of warm water that showered down upon them.

Michelle grabbed his hand and sucked his fingers into her mouth one by one. A low moan eased past Mark's lips. Pure, unadulterated lust coursed through them both and Michelle could no longer deny what she had been feeling for the man. She ran her hands across his body, lathering the line of each ripped muscle. The man was sheer joy and Michelle could only marvel that he was standing before her, his desire for her seeping like rain from his eyes.

After they'd soaped and rinsed each other off, each stroke followed by the brush of his lips or hers, they'd stepped from the shower, Mark wrapping her warmly in a plush white towel folded neatly atop the marble counter.

As she held his gaze, Mark suddenly swept her into his arms and carried her into the bedroom, laying her easily atop the quilt-covered mattress. He stared down at her, his gaze sweeping warmth across the length of her body. When Michelle reached her arms out to draw him to her, he eased his body gently atop hers. Flesh kissed flesh, the space between them growing warm as they met in another deep kiss. Mark nibbled her lips, sliding his tongue against hers as Michelle moaned pure pleasure into his mouth.

Paying homage to the sheer beauty of her, Mark stroked, kissed, licked and caressed every part of her body as Michelle lay back against the bed in awe of his skills. She was breathing heavily with wanting, perspiration dampening her towel-dried skin as heat raged from the center of her core. The man had her writhing with pleasure and, before Michelle realized what was happening, the first of many orgasms to come ripped through her body, causing her to quiver with complete abandonment beneath him. Mark smiled smugly, clearly amused by what he'd been able to accomplish.

The duo sank into an endless dance of lips, breath coming fast. Michelle could feel him swollen full and hard against her upper thigh as Mark ground himself against her body.

"Do you have another condom?" he whispered, a palm pressed warmly against his back.

Michelle nodded, leaning across the mattress to pull a box of prophylactics from her nightstand. She gestured for him to lay back beside her, toying with the protection between her fingers. She gave him a sly wink as she crawled above him, kissing a path from his chest down to his thighs. When her warm breath blew along the length of his member, Mark stiffened with anticipation, ripples of heat washing down from his head to his curled toes. He groaned, calling her name as if in prayer and then she sucked him in, her tongue bathing the length of him with pleasure. Just as Michelle was about to bring him to a point of no return, she rolled the condom onto the pulsating steel that was aching for release and dropped her own body down against his.

Mark's eyes flew open to stare up her, enthralled as Michelle rode him easily, her thighs parted wide around his pelvis. Her head was thrown back, her mouth parted slightly, her breath coming in heavy gasps. Mark clasped her around the buttocks, pushing himself deep inside her as he lifted his torso up to taste her mouth one more time. Michelle bucked wildly as Mark's teasing fingers stroked her bliss spot, teasing the swollen nub unabashedly. When he called her name, she opened her eyes to stare into his, the man's gaze commanding her attention. Michelle suddenly spasmed, Mark shuddering in ecstasy beneath her. The moment was telling, the two still staring deep into each other's eyes as they rode one wave of pleasure after another.

Chapter 17

Activity around the racetrack was fast and furious at best, racers and support crews prepping for the evening's activities. Michelle had arrived later than she'd wanted to, every muscle in her body deliciously relaxed. The time she and Mark had spent with each other still lingered down the length of her limbs, the flow of good feelings ebbing from her core.

Mark had called in to his office to say that he would be late, canceling his morning meetings without a second thought. Before Michelle could call in her schedule, Simon had been calling her, surprised that he had made it to the garage before she had. The couple was sure that they'd left a lot of people wondering what they were up to but neither was concerned, too absorbed in each other to care.

As Michelle stepped into the Rockman bays, bikes were lined in a neat row, the team's mechanics giving them one last check before the beginning eliminations started. The three men all turned to her with updates before she barked out quick orders to insure every ride was race ready.

On the other side of the pit area, Mark and his crew were reviewing his ride strategy, the man trying to assimilate the wealth of advice he was being given. His brothers, John and Luke, stood off to the side, arms folded across their chests, taking it all in.

"This is some spectacle," John was saying when Mark finally joined them, his helmet tucked beneath his arm.

Mark nodded. "It's going to be a good race. I can feel it."

Luke nodded. "Just be careful out there. We don't want anything to happen to you."

Mark gave his brother a light tap against his shoulder. "I'll be just fine. I can do this with my eyes closed and my hands tied behind my back."

John gave his brother a wry smirk. "I'm sure you can, just don't do it today. Be safe, not sorry."

"So," Luke said, looking around to see who might be listening to their conversation. "Matthew filled us in on you and my girl Mitch. How's that going?"

Mark grinned, his face gleaming with pure joy. "It's going very well. That woman is incredible!"

John nodded, lifting his hand to slap his brother's palm in a high five. "Told you love will turn you inside out and have you riding sky high!"

Luke rolled his eyes. "You two are seriously scaring me."

Mark chuckled. "Let's pass this curse on," he said. "Your turn is coming, little brother," he said, pointing in Luke's direction. "Just you wait. One of these days you're going to find a woman who'll have your head spinning."

Luke shuddered and threw his hands up. "Well, if that

happens, shoot me and put me out of my misery. There are just too many beautiful women with long legs and short skirts for me to chase. Why would I want to give any of that up?"

John smiled. "Because finding that one perfect pair of legs will be the best thing to ever happen to you."

Luke shuddered again and the trio burst out into warm laughter.

As they stood chatting easily together, Mark noticed the two detectives who were investigating the accidents moving from one race pit to the other. Both had stopped in the entrance of Rockman's team door, staring intently. Mark could feel himself stiffen, his earlier calm gone. Both of his brothers sensed the change in his demeanor.

"What's the matter, Mark?" John questioned, concern filling his words.

Mark sighed, shifting his helmet from one arm to the other. "I'm not sure." He gestured with his head. "Something about those two doesn't feel right."

"Who are they?" Luke asked.

"Police. Investigating those accidents here at the track."

John nodded again. "They still think Mitch had something to do with it?"

Mark shrugged, tossing his brother a quick glance. "She's high on the suspect list."

"That's not good," John said.

"No, it isn't. But Mitch didn't do anything wrong. I don't want them harassing her just because they think she did."

John shifted his hands into his pockets. "I can understand that," he said softly, still watching where Mark watched.

The trio continued to stare as the two police officers strolled casually away from the Rockman bays. All three noted when one of them stopped to have an intense conversation with Greg Rockman. The team's owner was smiling, his trademark gesture permanently plastered on his face.

"Now, that would surely be an unholy alliance there," Mark said to no one in particular.

John turned to stare at his brother. "They do seem well acquainted with each other, don't they?"

"Just let it go for now," Luke advised, glancing at the watch on his wrist. "It's almost time for you to run your first race. You need to be focused."

The three looked from one to the other, John nodding his head in assent. "Yeah, back to business. I've got a few side wagers on you. Don't disappoint me."

Mark grinned, slapping his brother on his back. "Oh, you'll win your money, big brother. I guarantee it!"

"Where's Matthew?" Luke suddenly asked, changing the subject.

"He and Vanessa disappeared an hour ago."

Rolling his eyes skyward, Mark laughed. "Vanessa is like a fly on the wall the way she hovers around here. There's no telling where she's dragged Matthew off to. Lord only knows what kind of trouble Vanessa is getting him in."

John laughed with him. "That's what I'm afraid of." He extended his closed fist and Mark pounded it lightly with his own as the two completed a boyhood ritual. "See you in the winner's box."

Mark pointed a finger in his brother's direction. "Bring the champagne!" he exclaimed as his brothers chuckled, moving to the door.

Minutes later Mark was easing his bike to the starting line for his first run. It was time to race.

Michelle had checked, double- and triple-checked each race bike for potential problems. As far as she was concerned there was nothing amiss, each of her riders prepared to do what they did best. Down in the pits, it was loud and dusty as a wealth of energy filled the air around her.

She'd had a quick moment with Mark before he'd had to go run his first heat, winning it easily. The two had shared a quick kiss before she'd had to go back to doing her job, reminded by Simon and a few others that fraternizing with the competition wasn't good business. Michelle had only laughed at the poor jokes the crowd had been making about the two of them and their divided loyalties. Personally Michelle was quite comfortable cheering them all on to victory.

Detective Daniels and his partner had been eyeing her from afar ever since she'd arrived. Michelle had been disconcerted at first, her uncle calming down her anxiety. "It's nothing," the old man had exclaimed. "They're just being nosy. That's how they do their job."

Michelle hadn't been convinced that nosy was what they were being. Even she hadn't missed the interaction with her team's owner, Rockman standing in deep conversation with both officers.

By the end of the evening Rockman Racing was going head-to-head with Team Stallion. Only one of Rockman's five bikes had made it to the final heat, the driver one of the best in the business. Mark Stallion had proved himself pro team worthy, riding with a skill and efficiency that put him heads above the rest. The ease with which he handled the machinery was like he'd been riding all of his life.

Michelle slipped over to the Stallion garage to wish him luck. "Watch yourself when you get to your midpoint," she said, her hands pressed warmly against his chest. "Shift your weight forward just a touch more and you'll get off the leg faster."

Mark nodded, leaning to press his lips to her lips. "We need to have a conversation about your employment. I could use your skills on my team."

"Yes, you could, but I like the team I work for."

"I promise you'll like this team more. You'll get fringe benefits," he said, raising his eyebrows suggestively.

"Didn't I hear you say something once about never mixing business with pleasure?"

"We wouldn't be. It's a fringe benefit, sort of like insurance and your pension."

Michelle laughed. "If you say so."

Mark hugged her, relishing the feel of her in his arms. "I do and I'm the boss."

Michelle nodded her head against his chest. "I've got to go. Have a good run and I'll see you later."

Detective Daniels caught her by the arm just before she made it back to the Rockman work bays. "Ms. Coleman, you need to come with us."

Michelle snatched her arm away from the man, tensing tightly. "What's this about now, Detective? Don't you see we're in the middle of a race? I really don't have time for this."

His partner grabbed Michelle's hand, twisting it harshly behind her back as he slapped a pair of handcuffs around her wrists. Before Michelle realized what was happening, the man was reading her Miranda rights.

"Michelle Coleman, you're under arrest. You have the right to remain silent. Anything you say can and will be held against you in a court of law. You have the right to an attorney. If you can't afford an attorney, one will be provided to you. Do you understand your rights as I have explained them to you?" the man queried nonchalantly.

A look of disbelief crossed Michelle's face. "You have to be kidding! What am I being charged with?"

Daniels smiled, guiding her toward the exit. "Attempted murder, Ms. Coleman. Attempted murder."

The Stallion-Briscoe family filled the VIP section of the viewing bleachers. With each heat, they'd been cheering loudly for Mark, excitement wafting like a heavy cloud above them.

"This is so exciting!" Marah exclaimed, leaning back against her husband's chest.

"That boy can ride that bike now!" Edward intoned.

Marah's sister Eden waved a hand in front of her face. "It's a little loud, don't you think?"

Marla laughed at her sibling. "Stop complaining and enjoy it. Mark may actually win this. How exciting would that be!"

Vanessa and Matthew laughed as Luke wrapped a warm arm around Eden's shoulder. He looked up at Eden's husband who was shaking his head in dismay. "Jack, you need to get your girl out more."

Jack Waller laughed. "Eden's idea of out is a five-star hotel and restaurant. My baby doesn't do rough and dirty and this is a little rough and dirty for her." He leaned to kiss his wife's forehead.

"I know that's right," Eden exclaimed. "This is too much for me." She rolled her eyes. "And I get out enough, thank you very much." She fanned herself with a copy of the evening's race program. "How much longer?" she asked curiously, her gaze skating back to the concrete track.

Vanessa smiled. "Not long. There's only one more race. Mark's made it to the finals."

"He'll win this," Edward exclaimed. "That other boy can't ride like Mark."

"Let's keep our fingers crossed," John said.

"We need to say a prayer or two," Juanita said as she moved back to her husband's side, a tray of drinks in her hands. "Beer, baby?"

Edward reached for his glass. "Y'all hear that joke about the Lone Ranger and Tonto?" the man asked, looking from one face to the others.

The Briscoe sisters both rolled their eyes, glancing at the Stallion brothers. Vanessa leaned forward in her seat. "No, sir, Mr. Briscoe. I've never heard it."

John laughed as Marah groaned out loud. "Leave your father alone, Marah. We all love his jokes."

Eden shook her head. "You haven't heard them every day since you were born. I'm the oldest. I've heard them more than everyone."

"Nothing wrong with a good laugh," Edward said, flipping a hand at his daughter. "You girls know you like my jokes."

Eden laughed. "Sure, Daddy!"

"Tell it, Mr. Briscoe," Vanessa implored. "I could use a laugh."

Edward grinned. "The Lone Ranger and Tonto walked into a bar and sat down to drink a beer. After a few minutes, a big tall cowboy walked in and said, 'Who owns the big white horse outside?' The Lone Ranger stood up, hitched his gun belt, and said, 'I do…why?' The cowboy looked at the Lone Ranger and said, 'I just thought you would like to know that your horse is about dead outside!' The Lone Ranger and Tonto rushed outside, and sure enough, Silver was ready to die from heat exhaustion. The Lone Ranger got the horse some cold water, and soon, Silver was starting to feel a little better. The Lone Ranger turned to Tonto and said, 'Tonto, I want you to run around Silver and see if you can create enough of a breeze to make him start to feel better.' Tonto answered, 'Sure,

Kemosabe,' and took off running circles around Silver. Not able to do anything else but wait, the Lone Ranger returned to the bar to finish his drink. A few minutes later, another cowboy struts into the bar and asks, 'Who owns that big white horse outside?' The Lone Ranger stands again, and claims, 'I do, what's wrong with him this time?' The cowboy looks him in the eye and says, 'Nothing, but you left your Injun runnin'."

Vanessa bust out laughing, the rest of the room joining in with her.

"You have to admit, Eden," Vanessa said. "That was funny!"

John moved from his seat to the viewing window. "Hey, the race is about to begin. Mark's at the starting line."

The family all moved to his vantage point. John tossed a glance toward his two brothers, warm smiles filling all their faces. Marah hugged him around the waist, leaning easily into his side. Vanessa stood with her fingers crossed, both hands raised out in front of her.

Silence filled the room as they strained to hear the announcer over the loudspeaker, the man introducing the final two riders and announcing the start of the race. Gazes were affixed on the electronic device they called the Christmas tree, with its multicolored starting lights. As the top lights of the tree lit up, indicating the riders were in place, approximately seven inches from the starting line, everyone took a collective breath and held it. The quiet in the room was suddenly palpable.

They watched as Mark eased his bike forward, the tree lighting the next set of lights indicating Mark was perfectly positioned on the starting line. John squeezed Marah's hand tightly and she squeezed back. A split second later the lights flashed from amber to green and both bikes shot off the starting line like they'd been fired out of a cannon.

184 *Tame a Wild Stallion*

The crowd and the engines both roared loudly, fans cheering with intensity as the big engines roared down the raceway. In the blink of an eye Mark was well on his way down the track and then seconds later, just as he reached the finish line, easily taking the victory, something went wrong.

The explosion was sudden and unexpected, the back end of Mark's bike igniting into flames. The crowd watched as the rear end of the vehicle seemed to flip forward, sending Mark harshly into the ground.

The moment was surreal as the rider and his bike appeared to be rolling head over heels in slow motion, both crashing into the concrete barrier at the end of the raceway. Vanessa gasped loudly, the entire family suddenly fighting to catch their breath. John moved first, rushing for the entrance and out the door, Matthew and Luke close on his heels. The color was drained from Juanita's face, fear having a tight grip on her chest. Marah grabbed her hand, pulling her along as they followed behind the men, Eden and Vanessa leading the way. And down below, the Stallion pit crew raced to their driver's side, the racetrack's emergency vehicles only a split second ahead of them.

Chapter 18

Michelle felt as if her heart was beating in multiple speeds, the organ beating so fast that she felt as if her chest were about to explode. It was unbearably warm in the small interrogation room they'd locked her in and she was feeling claustrophobic between the four walls. Perspiration beaded across her palms, brow and upper lip and her muscles felt as if they were convulsing in harsh tremors.

She was finding it exceedingly difficult to maintain control and it was taking everything within her to hold back the wealth of tears that pressed hot against the back of her eyelids. She wanted to cry and scream, but most of all she wanted to be in Mark's arms where she felt safe and protected.

She'd not yet been afforded her one telephone call and it felt as if she had been held hostage for hours. Twisting her hands together nervously, she couldn't begin to imagine what they could possibly be doing and how they'd come to the conclusion that she had even thought of murdering someone, let alone attempted it.

Pacing from corner to corner, Michelle imagined that it would take very little for her to have a complete and total meltdown, every ounce of her sanity dissipating in the too warm air.

Minutes later the detective with the not-so-warm personality entered the room. "Ms. Coleman, we'll be transferring you over to the women's correctional center to be processed."

"Don't I get a telephone call?"

The man nodded. "Yes. You do. You'll get to make that call after your paperwork has been completed."

Michelle tossed her hands up in exasperation. "This is truly ridiculous. You've made a horrible mistake."

The man shrugged. "That's not how we see it, Ms. Coleman." The man placed a tape recorder onto the table. "Would you like to make a statement now, Ms. Coleman?"

She rolled her eyes in frustration. "I'll make a statement to my attorney as soon as I can place that call."

The two stood staring at each other, annoyance wafting between them. Michelle would have given anything to have been able to knock the smug expression off the detective's face. Instead, she heaved a deep sigh and dropped down onto the hard wooden chair that sat before the metal table.

The detective pushed the stop button on the recorder and picked it up. "I'll be back momentarily," he said, moving back to the door.

Michelle shrugged, refusing to respond. It was clear the duo was trying to get to her, to wear down her defenses, but she wasn't going to let them get the best of her. Michelle knew that all she had to do was hold on a little longer and Mark would do everything to make the worst of this go far away.

* * *

John Stallion sat with his head in his hands. He couldn't believe they were going through this again, memories of their hospital vigil for his wife Marah high on this thought list. Much time had passed since Marah had been thrown by her favorite horse, the massive animal spooked by a rattlesnake while the two had been out riding. Marah had recovered nicely, barely a scar to show for her numerous injuries, and now, here they were, waiting for news about Mark.

Mark had been unconscious, an ambulance rushing him to the hospital. His family had been right behind them, arriving minutes after the emergency vehicle. John's fraternity brother, Dr. Marcus Shepherd had met them in the emergency room entrance, rushing behind the gurney as they'd wheeled Mark into an examination room. Now John and his kinfolk were sitting in wait of information, praying that Mark would be well.

Edward pressed a large hand to John's shoulder. The two men locked gazes, neither needing to say a word, both sending prayer skyward as fast as they could form the litany.

Luke, who'd gone to make a telephone call, came rushing inside, moving right to John's side. His brother gestured for him to take a seat, sensing that something else had Luke in turmoil.

"What's wrong?" John asked, his voice dropping so that only Luke could hear him.

Luke glanced around then leaned in to his brother, the gesture conspiratorial. John repeated his question. "What's happened?"

"They arrested Mitch. When she didn't come here to the hospital I knew something was wrong. Her uncle says the police took her away right before Mark's race. She probably doesn't even know about the accident."

"Who did you call?"

"No one yet. I wanted to speak with you first."

The older sibling rose to his feet, strolling across the room and out into the hallway. Luke followed behind him, Matthew trailing along curiously.

"What's going on?" Matthew questioned, looking from one to the other.

"They arrested Mark's girl. She's been charged with attempted murder," Luke answered.

Matthew shook his head. "That's not good."

John nodded his agreement. "No, it's not good at all and this is surely not the time for us to have to deal with it."

Luke crossed his arms over his chest. "No, it isn't, but Mark would expect us to. He loves Mitch. If it were Marah you would expect us to take care of her if you couldn't."

John met Luke's stare. Matthew interjected. "Call our attorney. They already know what's going on. Mark's already hired them to help Mitch. They'll take care of it."

John reached into his pocket and pulled a crisp business card from the inside folds. "She'll need bail. We'll guarantee whatever she needs. Tell them to get her out today. If Mark needs her, I want to be sure she's there for him."

Luke nodded and did an about-face. Before he could head back down the hall, Dr. Shepherd appeared. The man's blank expression caused them all to stiffen with apprehension. Matthew pressed a nervous hand against John's back, the two brothers taking a step in the doctor's direction.

Marcus smiled. It was just a faint bend to his lips, barely noticeable if one hadn't been looking for it.

"How is he?" they all asked in unison.

Dr. Shepherd nodded. "He's going to be just fine. He's got a mild concussion and a lot of bruising but nothing a little rest and relaxation won't cure easily."

John blew a sigh of relief, anxiety lifting like a sweet

morning sunrise, a prayer of thanks spilling out of his mouth. Luke and Matthew were clasped in a warm embrace, hugging each other tightly. John moved to join them, wrapping his thick arms around both pairs of shoulders.

"Can we see him?" he asked, looking over Luke's shoulder at his friend.

Dr. Shepherd said, "Just a couple of you at a time. And we're going to keep him overnight for observation. He should be well enough to leave in the morning."

"Thank you, Marcus," John said, reaching for the man's hand and shaking it. "Thank you very much."

Dr. Shepherd nodded again. "Hey, buddy, let's get together for drinks or dinner the next time. I don't want to see you or your family in my hospital again."

John chuckled. "I'll do whatever I can, Marcus. I'd definitely prefer to see you over a shot of Scotch and a steak than meet you here again."

John watched the doctor disappear down the hallway and out of sight.

Matthew tapped him warmly against the back. "I'll go tell the others. You head on down to see Mark," he said firmly. "Luke, make those calls. When Mark starts asking for Mitch she should be here."

Luke grinned. "I'm on it!" he exclaimed as he headed in the opposite direction.

The two brothers stood watching behind him and then without another word, Matthew moved back into the waiting room to deliver the good news and John went to see that his baby brother was indeed doing just fine.

The whole family was gathered inside Mark's hospital room. A frantic young nurse had pleaded with them to leave, finally giving up when no one would pay her any attention. Laughter rang through the air as Mark's brothers gave him a hard time, each one cracking a joke about him winning the race on his head.

Each time he laughed Mark grabbed his skull with both hands, a raging headache shooting bullets behind his eyes. "Oh, oh, oh," Mark exclaimed. "That hurts. Don't make me laugh, guys!"

Matthew chuckled. "We're just glad you didn't hurt anything you might need later on," the man said teasingly.

Mark winced as mirth bubbled up from inside him, spilling out into the room.

Juanita held up a palm. "Okay, people. Mark needs to get some rest. We can all come back to visit him later." She leaned to kiss the man's cheek. "You get some sleep, Mark. That's an order."

Mark tossed the matriarch a quick salute. Juanita smiled as she bent to kiss him one more time.

"Thank you, Aunt Juanita," Mark said softly.

One by one the family marched out of the room, each of them stopping to hug and kiss the man good-night. When no one was left but John, Luke and Matthew, Mark sat upright, anxious for answers.

"Do they know what happened?" Mark asked, looking toward John.

His brother shrugged. "No, not yet, but they're investigating."

"What about the NHRA? Did they recognize my win?"

Matthew nodded. "It's unofficial pending a review, but that trophy definitely belongs to you."

Luke shook his head, confusion flooding his face. "What do they have to review?"

Mark sighed. "I imagine it's that post-run inspection. They

usually weigh the bike and check the fuel after each race and do a complete engine teardown if they think it's necessary."

The Stallion men looked from one to the other. John shook his head. "Well, there's no engine left for them to tear down, Mark. Your bike was incinerated. They don't have anything to weigh but ash."

Mark shook his head, leaning his back against the cushions of pillows. "Did anyone call Mitch for me?" he asked, looking at John. "Why isn't she here?"

John cut a glance toward Luke who turned to stare at Matthew. Mark immediately knew something was wrong.

"What?" he queried as he leaned forward. "Where's Mitch?"

Matthew sighed before answering. "She was arrested just before your race."

Shock registered on Mark's face. "Arrested? For what? What did she do?"

"They've charged her with attempted murder for the previous accidents at the racetrack."

"That's ridiculous," Mark shouted, his voice rising harshly. "Mitch didn't do anything to anyone."

"We're working on getting her out right now," Luke said, moving closer to his brother's bedside. "It's taking some time because the police believe she may have had something to do with your accident as well."

Mark tossed the stark white covers from around his legs and slid off the side of the hospital mattress.

"What are you doing?" John asked, a hand pressing hard against Mark's shoulder. "Where do you think you're going?"

"I'm going to go get Mitch."

"You can't leave the hospital, Mark. You have a concussion, remember?" John's incredulous expression met his brother's determined stare.

Mark tossed them all an icy look. "Mitch needs me right now and that's more important than anything else. Once she's home and safe I'll gladly come back to this hospital bed, but until then you can either help me or you can get out of my way. But I'm going and I'm going now!"

Michelle would have sworn before a judge and a jury that a whole day had passed since the detective had last entered the small room. The temperature had risen to an all-time high. No one had bothered to bring the bottle of water she'd politely asked for, and now her bladder was about to bust a gasket. Michelle couldn't begin to believe this was happening to her.

Rising from her seat, she knocked on the locked door. Tapping the toe of her steel-toed work boots against the concrete floor, she stood with attitude registered in her body language, her arms crossed over her chest in anger, as she waited for someone to come to her aid.

"Excuse me! Hello? Is anyone out there?"

Before she could knock a second time Detective Daniels pushed his way into the room. "Is there a problem, Ms. Coleman?"

"I need a restroom, please. And I would like to call my attorney."

The man eyed her for a brief moment, then stepped out of her path as he gestured toward a door at the end of the hallway. "The restroom is there," he said, pointing his index finger. "I'll be right outside so don't get any ideas."

Michelle shook her head and laughed. "You've been watching too many cops-and-robbers movies, Detective. I'm innocent. I don't need to try anything," she said.

The man didn't bother to answer as Michelle pushed her

way past him, closing the ladies' room door securely behind her. Once she'd relieved herself, pausing to press a damp paper towel to the back of her neck and splash cold water over her face, she met Detective Daniels back out in the hall. The man returned her to the cramped enclosure for questioning.

"What's going on, Detective?" Michelle asked. "Why is this taking so long?"

He smiled, the gesture annoying Michelle to no end. As far as she was concerned there was nothing for either of them to be smiling about.

"The city of Dallas extends its apology for the inconvenience," he answered sarcastically.

Michelle rolled her eyes, moving back to the seat the detective pointed her to. Her bad mood was evident as she crossed her arms in front of her, leaning back against the wooden chair harshly.

The man sat down in front of her. He laid a large manila folder on the desktop, flipping through the pages as if he were looking for something special. Michelle's gaze never left the man's face as she feigned disinterest in what he was doing.

"Ms. Coleman, were you in the vicinity of the Stallion team's garage at any time today?" the man suddenly asked as he met her stare.

The question was unexpected, raising Michelle's curiosity. "Excuse me?"

"Today. Were you in the Stallion team's garage at any time?"

"Yes. Why?"

"Were you ever there alone?"

"No."

"Why were you there at all?"

Michelle sighed. "I went to wish Mr. Stallion good luck before his race."

"Do you always visit your competitors' garages to wish them luck?"

"No, not always."

There was a lengthy pause as Daniels went back to searching his folder. A minute later he laid a color photograph in front of her, the glossy eight-by-ten inch image of a demolished motorcycle staring back at her.

"Do you recognize that bike, Ms. Coleman?"

Michelle pulled the photo into her hands and stared at it. She dropped it back to the table. "There really isn't much left to recognize, is there, Detective?"

The man nodded his blond head. "That was Mark Stallion's motorcycle. It blew up with him on it this evening. You wouldn't know anything about that now? Would you, Ms. Coleman?"

Michelle gasped, snatching the picture back from the desktop. Her hands were shaking noticeably as she stared again. She tossed the picture back at the detective. "Where's Mark? Is he all right? Was he hurt?" Michelle asked, her questions coming with a rush of breath.

Detective Daniels didn't bother to answer, standing back up on his feet. He gathered his folder and the photo, then turned back toward the room's only door. Michelle's eyes were wide with fright, her cheeks flaming red with rage. She heard herself screaming after the man, unable to maintain her cool. "Don't you walk away! What's happened to Mark? You have to tell me!"

At the door, Detective Daniels paused, turning to meet her frightened gaze. "I'm sorry, Ms. Coleman," he said before he exited the room, the door closing behind him. "This just isn't your lucky day."

Chapter 19

Time felt like it was ticking even slower, moving at a snail's pace. By the time the door finally swung back open Michelle was on the verge of hysteria. She was past ready to rage at the first soul who stepped through the entrance.

When Mark limped over the threshold, extending his arms out toward her, Michelle's frustrations burst forth like a plug pulled from a dam. Tears spilled down her cheeks, rolling off her chin as she broke down crying. Moving around the table to her side, Mark wrapped his arms tightly around her. Michelle stiffened slightly, shock filtering through her senses and then she fell against him, sobbing uncontrollably, her fingers clutching the front of his white T-shirt.

Pressing a gentle kiss to the top of her head, Mark held her and allowed her to cry. He just knew that Michelle was not a woman who cried easily and the fact that she was sobbing so unabashedly, completely disregarding his brothers, attorney and the police officer who'd entered behind him, told him that this was a cry Michelle desperately needed. His large palms danced slowly up and down her back, the soothing caresses meant to calm her.

"It's okay, baby," he whispered softly. "Everything's going to be okay," he said, holding her tighter.

Michelle nodded her head against his chest, believing for the first time since she'd been arrested that things could truly be okay.

Michelle looked up at him, her eyes meeting his. "They said you blew up," she sputtered, choking on the sobs that still consumed her. "They said," she started before the words caught in her throat, her crying gaining control.

Mark chuckled. "Well, it was close but I'm still here. I've got to buy me a new motorcycle though. Toasted my ride at the finish line."

Michelle clutched him tighter. "I thought I'd lost you and no one would tell me anything," she gasped loudly, starting to sob all over again.

"Baby girl, you will never lose me. I'm not going anywhere," he said, smoothing her hair with his palm. "I love you too much to ever leave you," he added, his voice dropping low against her ear. "I love you, Mitch." Tilting her face upward, Mark pressed his mouth to her lips and kissed her.

Behind them, John and Matthew were both shaking their heads. John cleared his throat loudly, drawing attention to the crowd gathered around them. Mark looked up, suddenly remembering that he wasn't alone. He'd been so consumed with getting to Michelle and insuring she was well that he'd completely forgotten the family that had joined him. He laughed, heat warming his cheeks, then turned to smile back at Michelle.

"You two ready to go?" John asked, looking from one to the other. "We need to get you back to bed, Mark," he said firmly.

Michelle's eyes widened with surprise. "What...why...?"

"He checked himself out of the hospital without permission," Matthew explained. "His doctor's not happy. Mark has severe bruising and a mild concussion."

Michelle pressed one palm to his abdomen as she wrapped her other arm around his back. "I can't believe you. Why would you do something like that?"

Mark shrugged. "You were more important than a concussion."

The police officer knocked against the door. "Okay, people. Y'all need to take this lovefest someplace else."

"Gladly," Mark said, dropping his arm around Michelle's shoulders.

"I can leave?" Michelle asked, looking toward the attorney.

The man nodded his head. "Yes. Mark posted your bail, but it comes with one contingency."

Michelle frowned. "What's that?"

"You've been released into Mark's custody and he's personally responsible for you. He'll need to know where you are at all times."

Michelle paused, turning to stare back up at the man. Mark swiped his thumb over her cheeks, brushing away the moisture that still lingered on her skin. "I've had them ready one of the guest rooms for you at the house. Is that okay with you, Mitch?" Mark questioned.

Nodding, Michelle didn't bother to speak, agreeing to anything that would put this day behind her and keep her close to the man she loved.

* * *

Everyone was waiting at the Preston Hollow home for them to return. Inside the cherry-paneled library, Edward and Simon sat in conversation, the old-timers becoming well acquainted with each other. Juanita was pacing the floor nervously, walking a worn path on the Oriental carpet that decorated the floor. Marah sat with her infant nephew balanced against her knees as her sisters engaged in deep conversation with Luke. Their husbands stood staring at the billiards table, both studying their respective shots while they passed the time away.

A limousine dropped them all off at the entrance to the property. Mark pulled Michelle along beside him as he welcomed her to his home for the first time. Michelle took in the expansive view, her eyes skating back and forth as she stared in awe. She couldn't begin to find the words to explain what she was feeling at that moment.

"It's not as stuffy as it looks," Mark said, bemused by her expression.

Michelle shook her head from side to side. "It's so big!" she exclaimed.

Mark and his brothers laughed.

"It just looks that way," one of the men answered.

"It's really quite cozy," another added.

"You'll get use to it," Mark said, clasping her hand beneath his and squeezing it gently. "It's going to be your home until we get this mess settled, and then…" Mark paused raising his eyebrows suggestively.

"Then what?" Michelle queried.

Mark shrugged, a wry smile filling his dark face. "Who knows, maybe I'll be able to convince you to stay."

Michelle was momentarily overwhelmed by the noise and commotion. She'd never experienced so much family in one place at one time before. Everyone seemed to be talking and laughing all at once and she didn't know where to focus her attention first. Mark made the formal introductions before Juanita forced him to take a seat, the matriarch clearly not pleased to see him up and out of the hospital.

"I declare," the woman admonished. "I have half a mind to turn you right over my knee and give you a good spanking," she said, pressing a cool palm to his forehead.

"We'd all like to see that!" Edward exclaimed. "Yessiree boy! That would sure 'nuff be some sight to see."

Everyone in the room laughed.

"I'm too big for that, Aunt Juanita," Mark chuckled.

"I wouldn't be so sure of that," John interjected.

"Me neither," Luke added. "As I recall..."

Mark held up a bandaged hand, stalling his brother's comment. "Don't listen to them, Mitch. They all tell lies."

Michelle laughed. "Do they really?"

Mark nodded. "Yes. Do you want to know how you can tell when they're fibbing?"

"How?"

"Their lips move."

Michelle laughed heartily, the others joining in.

"Now you know that's not true," Luke said.

"I know that's right," Matthew added. "Mitch, everything we'll tell you about Mark will be the truth. The whole truth and nothing but the truth."

"So help us, God!" the other two brothers chimed in unison.

Mark laughed. "Y'all haven't been that in sync since never," he said warmly.

Juanita shook her head. "I swear, you boys don't ever stop."

"As bad as my girls!" Edward said, moving to wrap an arm around his wife's shoulders.

The Briscoe sisters all rolled their eyes skyward.

"What are you trying to say, Daddy?" Marah queried.

"I said it, pumpkin. Y'all just as bad as these boys."

Marla, Marah's twin, shook her head.

"Please, don't get him started."

Eden giggled. "We'll be here all night if you do."

"No, we won't," her husband Jack interjected, rising to his feet. "Some of us have to work tomorrow."

"I know that's right," John declared. He looked toward Matthew and Luke. "And Mark is the only Stallion who's getting a sick day tomorrow."

"And the day after," Mark added.

Juanita leaned down to hug him. "Take the rest of the week, baby. You need you some rest. Mitch, I'm putting you in charge," the older woman proclaimed.

Mitch nodded, encouraged by the wealth of warm expressions that turned to stare at her. Family felt good and she could see herself getting used to it.

Simon moved to his niece's side, wrapping Michelle in a tight embrace. "They didn't give you too hard a time down there, did they?" he asked, the question laced with concern.

A noticeable frown crossed her expression as she shook her head. Her voice came soft and low. "I'm sure it could have been worse," she said with a quick shrug.

Mark gestured for her to join him, his index finger waving her to sit beside him. As Michelle settled against him, he hugged her tightly. "It will never happen again. I promise you that, baby," he said, pressing a damp kiss to her forehead. "Never."

Juanita pressed a palm to each one's shoulder and squeezed gently. "We're going to make sure you both are just fine," she said. She leaned one last time to kiss them both.

"Thank you, Aunt Juanita," Mark said softly.

Juanita pointed an index finger skyward. "You two head

on up to bed. You both need some rest. Michelle, I readied the room right next to Mark's. Make yourself comfortable. This is your home now. Your uncle brought over some of your things and the housekeeper can get anything else you might need. Don't hesitate to ask."

Michelle smiled. "Thank you," she said as she and Mark both came to their feet. After hugging and kissing everyone, the couple headed up the stairs, good-nights ringing in the air behind them as the family retreated out, heading to their re-spective homes.

Chapter 20

There wasn't one clock in the oversize bedroom. Michelle didn't have a clue what time it was or how long she'd been sleeping. The last thing she recalled was Mark curling his body around hers, groaning softly as a pinch of pain pulled at his bruised muscles. Minutes later the man's prescription drugs had kicked in with a vengeance and he was snoring softly into her ear. The soft drone of his breath had been a welcome balm, lulling her into a deep, comfortable slumber.

Mark was still curled warmly around her, the heat from his body blanketing her own. Michelle closed her eyes, savoring the touch of Mark's broad chest against her back. His fingers had glided across her tummy and breasts throughout the night, gentle caresses that had left her feeling full and warm inside, and even in his sleep he'd leaned in to kiss the back of her neck, nuzzling his face into her hair.

With the rising sun the hint of a morning erection had

pressed heavy against her buttocks and Michelle couldn't help smiling to herself. Making love hadn't been on either's mind the night before, both falling out with exhaustion. As well, Michelle imagined Mark's injuries might necessitate them abstaining for a while. But the man was slowly grinding himself against her backside, his breathing deepening as he pressed himself against her.

Turning, Michelle rolled over to face him. As she did, Mark opened one eye and smiled sweetly down at her.

"Wow!" Mark exclaimed softly. "You are so beautiful in the morning."

Michelle smiled back. "So are you. Good morning."

"Good morning, sweetie. Did you sleep okay?"

She nodded. "Hmm. I did. How about you?"

"I did, too. I always sleep well when I'm with you."

"Your aunt Juanita might not like that I slept in your bed last night and not the guest room."

Mark chuckled. "I won't tell her if you don't tell her. Besides, having you close was the best medicine for me."

Michelle grinned. "I just bet it was."

Mark winced ever so slightly.

"Are you all right?" Michelle asked, worry washing over her.

"Just a little sore," he said as he eased over onto his back. He pressed a heavy hand against his crotch. "I also have a little personal problem," he said with a quick laugh.

"Doesn't look like your personal problem is that little," Michelle giggled.

Mark laughed with her. "Mitch has jokes!"

Michelle pressed her hand against the waistband of his pajamas, easing her fingers inside. She slowly trailed her hands across the taut muscles, curling his pubic hair around her fingers until she reached the length of pulsating steel that strained full and taut for her attention. When she wrapped her palm around him, Mark gasped out loud.

"Girl, you're starting something!"

"No," Michelle said teasingly. "I'm going to finish something."

"Oh, baby," Mark groaned softly as Michelle tightened her grip around his shaft, the appendage jumping beneath her touch. Pleasuring him was all Michelle could think about, wanting to ease the pressure she knew he was feeling. She slowly moved her hand up and down, stroking him gently, the pace slow and easy. Mark moaned his satisfaction, Michelle's name ringing softly off the tip of his tongue.

Parting his legs to allow her easier access, Mark relished the sensation of Michelle tugging and pulling at his manhood. His breathing became even heavier as she ran an index finger over his testicles before stroking him harder and faster. With every stroke his nerve endings quivered with pleasure, his whole body feeling invigorated. Michelle's ministrations were unbelievably sweet, making him completely forget the injuries that were causing him some brief hurt.

With a deep exhalation, Mark's body suddenly shook, contraction after contraction shaking his large frame. He held his breath, his hips bucking with each burst of pleasure as Michelle brought him to orgasm, her fingers continuing to massage his member. When he recovered, the last quiver of ecstasy causing his toes to curl, a wide grin filled his face.

"So, how's your morning going?" Michelle asked, her eyebrows raised, a look of bemusement crossing her face.

Mark nodded. "Girl, what you do to me!" he exclaimed.

Michelle laughed softly as Mark pulled Michelle close, hugging her tightly. He nuzzled his face into her neck, one hand teasing the lace that edged her bikini-style panties.

"I owe you," he whispered into her ear, trailing his tongue along the line of her lobe.

Michelle giggled, grabbing his wrist with her hand to stall his teasing. "Yes, you do and I'll collect later. Right now I need a shower and some breakfast," she said firmly.

Mark kissed her cheek. "I can do breakfast. Pancakes and bacon work for you?"

"With maple syrup?"

"Is there any other way?" Mark said with a wide smile.

"Then what?" Michelle queried, sitting upright in the bed. She pulled her legs to her chest, wrapping her arms around her knees.

Mark sat up beside her, pressing his lips to her shoulder and kissing the soft flesh gently. "Then I suggest we crawl back into this bed and stay here for the rest of the day. How does that sound?"

Michelle smiled, her eyes glistening with joy. "Like the perfect plan!"

Three whole days passed with neither one of them thinking about leaving Mark's room or his bed. The loyal staff that managed the family home insured meals were brought up whenever either of them had a request and not once did they want for anything. Mark and Michelle became lost in each other, oblivious to everything and everyone on the other side of the closed door.

Both were dozing comfortably when an insistent knock disturbed the peace and quiet they'd made for themselves. Mark opened one eye, pretending to ignore the harsh tapping that had woken him from a very sweet dream. Michelle rolled against him, her own eyes fluttering open and then closed.

"Someone wants you," she mumbled, barely coherent.

Mark blew a deep sigh. "I thought we put out a Do Not Disturb sign."

Michelle smiled, fighting not to fall back into a state of slumber. "I told you that wasn't going to work but for so long."

The rapping at the door came louder, someone on the other side desperate for their attention.

"Who is it?" Mark finally called out, lifting his body upward.

"It's me," Vanessa answered from the other side. "Open the door. What are you two doing in there?"

Mark tossed Michelle a look as he waved his head from side to side. "Go away, Vanessa."

His friend laughed, banging against the door for the umpteenth time. "No. Open up. It's important."

Mark sighed, turning to stare down at Michelle. "Make her go away."

Michelle laughed. "You better open the door and talk to her. Otherwise I think she might camp out there and that wouldn't be pretty."

The man rolled his eyes. "What do you want, Vanessa? I'm busy right now."

"I just bet you are. But I don't want you. I want to talk to Mitch."

Mitch's eyes blew open, her gaze meeting Mark's. Mark's expression was priceless. "Something I should know about?" he said teasingly.

Michelle laughed. "I don't have a clue," she said, moving to lift her naked body upward. She reached for the terry bathrobe that rested at the foot of the bed, wrapping it around her body. Mark pulled the covers up to his waist, sitting back against the padded headboard and the mound of pillows that had rested beneath his head.

"Come on in, Vanessa," he said, the words barely out before

the doorknob was turning and the woman was pushing her way inside.

"I swear," Vanessa exclaimed, a wide smile pulling from ear to ear. "Folks is starting to talk about you two. Miss Juanita is about to have a fit but John and Mr. Edward won't let her bother you." Vanessa plopped her body down against the bed, still grinning at her two friends. "So, what's up?"

Michelle laughed. "Good morning, Vanessa."

"More like good evening. It's almost five o'clock. You two planning to come up for air anytime soon?"

"What do you want with us, Vanessa?" Mark asked, pretending to be annoyed.

"First," she said, tossing an oversize backpack onto the mattress. "Your uncle Simon wanted me to give this to you. He thought you might need some clean clothes by now. Not that you've been wearing much," Vanessa muttered under her breath.

Mark tossed her a look that said he wasn't amused.

Vanessa was still grinning. "My bad. Okay now. He also said to tell you that more flowers were delivered to the garage for you." Vanessa passed her a stack of gift cards. "Girlfriend, you've been a busy little bee. I know Mark didn't send you no flowers but someone is trying to get your attention. You go, girl!"

Michelle took the stack of signed cards from Vanessa's hand, briefly flipping through them. The signatures were all the same, her secret admirer sending his love.

"This is starting to freak me out," she said, passing the stack to Mark.

"It's starting to piss me off," Mark said, his annoyance creasing the lines in his forehead. "We need to figure out who they're from and set him straight."

Vanessa laughed. "I do believe my boy is jealous! This is

going to be so funny in a few years," she said. "I can't wait to tell your children."

Mark shook his head. "Vanessa, go away."

The woman nodded, lifting her body off the bed. "Okay. But one more thing."

"What?"

"You two seem to have forgotten that Mitch isn't out of the woods just yet. The boys in blue have been down at the tracks trying real hard to get her convicted, but I've eavesdropped on a conversation or two that you two might be interested in."

Both Mark and Michelle sat up straighter. "What? What did you hear?" they asked in unison.

Vanessa backed her way to the door, her smile still filling her face. "I'll be in the library. I'll see you two downstairs when you're ready to talk 'cause this is just a little too freaky for my blood," she said, gesturing at them and the bed with her hands. She tossed them both a quick wink before easing out the door. "Bye!" Vanessa chimed as she closed the door behind her.

Mark and Michelle turned to face each other. Michelle suddenly laughed out loud. "I don't know who's crazier, her or us."

Mark laughed with her. "We'll figure it out later. Right now, let's get dressed. I think our playtime is officially over."

Showered and shaved, Mark made it downstairs to the library first, Michelle joining him minutes later. Vanessa was in deep conversation on her cell phone when the two stepped into the room. Simon was resting in an oversize wing chair, tapping his foot anxiously. A wide grin spilled across his face the minute he saw Michelle, and he jumped from his seat to wrap her in a warm embrace.

"Mitch! Girl, I was starting to worry about you," the man exclaimed excitedly. "Are you okay?"

Michelle hugged him back. "I'm just fine, Uncle Simon. Mark's been taking good care of me."

Simon tossed Mark a look, smiling his approval. He extended his hand to shake Mark's. "Thank you."

Smiling, Mark nodded. "Not a problem, sir. I won't let anything happen to our girl."

"I had my doubts about you at first," Simon said, his arm still wrapped around Michelle's shoulder. "But you've got me convinced. And I can see that my baby girl here loves you. That makes you all right in my book, son."

"I appreciate that, sir," Mark answered, his gaze sweeping from Simon's face to Michelle's and back again.

"Just you remember, Mitch is some sort of special. You do anything to hurt her and I will hurt you. You hear me?"

Mark chuckled. "Loud and clear."

Michelle laughed, moving to press a kiss to her uncle's face. "It's okay, Uncle Simon. I don't think you or I have anything to worry about."

Vanessa closed her cell phone and joined in the laughter. "No, sir. Mark's a good guy. Kind of dopey every now and then but what man isn't."

Mark rolled his eyes skyward. "Okay, Vanessa, so what is it you just had to tell us?" he asked, moving to change the subject.

"Mitch didn't do it."

"Well, we know that. Tell us something we don't know."

"I think I know who did."

Vanessa suddenly had all of their attention, everyone focused on every word coming out of her mouth. Mark gestured to the sofa, indicating that they should all take a seat. Simon dropped back into his wing chair. Mark sat in the

center of the leather ottoman as Michelle and Vanessa both
sat down on the matching sofa across from him.

"Go on," Mark said, coaxing Vanessa to continue.

Vanessa turned to Michelle. "You've been asking a lot of
questions about your father's accident. That's had a lot of
people talking about the past. Did you know your father and
Greg Rockman fell out with each other just before he died?"

Michelle bristled. "No. That's not true. I know they shared
a somewhat rocky relationship but they were very close.
They'd been friends for years."

"Well," Vanessa continued, shrugging her shoulders with
indifference, "from what I've heard, *close* wasn't that close."

Michelle turned her attention toward Simon. "Uncle
Simon, do you know anything about this?"

The old man sighed, suddenly drifting off into thought. His
expression was tense, lines of worry creasing his aged complexion. "I know Rockman and your father bumped heads a
time or two," Simon said. His gaze met Michelle's. "I heard
some rumors but I wasn't but so sure about any of them."

"What rumors?" Michelle queried.

"About your mother."

"My mother? What about my mother?"

"Well, I heard Rockman had a thing for your mother,"
Vanessa chimed in. "Seems that your mom was dating
Rockman and your father and left Rockman high and dry and
Rockman didn't like it one bit," the woman said, barely taking
a breath to get the words out. "They say it was some mess back
then since the two of them were best friends."

"Who said all this?" Mark asked.

Vanessa shrugged again. "Some of the old guys."

"Well, none of them ever said it to me," Mitch said.

Simon nodded. "They wouldn't. Ain't none of them

would want you to know about that, Mitch. It happened a long time ago."

"And that's not all," Vanessa continued. "The detective investigating your case has some history with Greg Rockman. I overheard the two of them talking right before you were arrested. Me and Matthew were down in the back of the..." Vanessa paused, her face flushing profusely. "Well, that's really not important," she said, waving a hand in front of her. "Anyway, the cop was saying he'd done his job and Rockman was saying he wasn't done with him yet. Then the cop said that Rockman didn't pay him enough to do whatever it was he wanted done and Rockman said the guy owed him big. They said some other stuff, too, but then the two of them saw us and stopped talking." Vanessa finally paused to take a deep breath.

"I swear, Vanessa!" Mark exclaimed, shaking his head.

Michelle tossed up her hands. "This is ridiculous. My mother left us. She didn't leave us to be with Uncle Greg. Uncle Greg has never been anything but kind toward me and my father."

"Rockman was in love with your mother," Simon said softly, leaning forward in his seat, his hands cupped in prayer before him. "We all knew it. Your father knew it, too. In fact, I know he and your Aunt Dorothy, bless her soul, talked about it a few times. Your mother didn't feel the same about him though. She loved your father when she could love someone. When things went bad between them two and she left, Rockman took it harder than your daddy did. Something like that can make a man do some strange things, Mitch."

Michelle rose from her seat, pacing the floor. "This doesn't make any sense to me. Not an ounce of sense. My mother was gone for years when my father died. What reason would Daddy and Uncle Greg have to argue about her then? Neither one of them had her so what difference did it make?" She looked from Vanessa to Simon and then let her gaze rest on Mark.

Vanessa shrugged. "Maybe they didn't fall out about your mother, Mitch. Maybe they fell out about you?"

Simon cringed. "Your Aunt Dorothy never did like that man being around you, Mitch. Something about him didn't make her happy. Your daddy told her she was fanning flames about nothing and then…" The man stopped speaking, drifting off into thought.

"Then what?" Michelle queried.

"Then Brent had his accident," the man concluded, his voice dropping to a loud whisper.

Mark looked at Simon. "Sir, do you think Rockman could have been responsible for Mr. Coleman's accident?" He tossed Michelle a quick look.

Simon inhaled a deep breath before answering. "Most of us have thought Rockman could have had something to do with it. I don't see him having cut that line on his own, but anything is possible."

"What about the other accidents?" Mark asked.

Simon shrugged. "Rockman definitely had more to gain than Mitch did."

"And if they blame Mitch for the last few accidents and she gets jail time for them, then he doesn't have to worry about anyone asking any more questions about her father's accident," Vanessa interjected. "He wins and all his problems go away."

Michelle jumped out of her seat in frustration, wrapping her arms tightly around her torso. "This is crazy. Uncle Greg would never do anything like that. Never."

Mark moved to her side, wrapping his arms around her. She met his gaze, holding it as warm tears brimmed at the edges of her eyes. "Crazy or not, baby, we need to find out the truth.

If he did do it, then anything is possible. Rockman doesn't like to lose anything. Maybe eliminating his competition has become a bad habit for him."

Chapter 21

He'd been sitting outside her home for two days and there was no sign of Michelle coming or going. Rockman's frustration was raging as he checked the time on his wristwatch for the umpteenth time. He'd seen her leave the police station with Stallion, the man arriving just minutes before he himself had been ready to show up and save the day. He'd been more than ready to play the hero, saving Michelle from the torture she'd had to endure and then Stallion had arrived, posting her bail before Rockman could get through the police station door.

Rockman had underestimated Stallion and the hold he had on Michelle. It had become clear that the two were closer than he'd realized and now he found himself wishing that Stallion's accident had been more permanent.

Mark Stallion and his brothers had always been a thorn in Rockman's side. A business deal gone bad had left a mountain of bad blood between them, their do-good attitude grating on

Rockman's last nerve. Rockman wasn't in business to make friends and he didn't give a rat's tail about the enemies he'd made either. Rockman was in business to make money and he didn't take kindly to anyone cutting into his earnings no matter the reason.

The Stallions hadn't seen things his way, threatening his profit margin, and he'd been forced to do what had been necessary to protect his goods. Stallion still held a grudge and now he was threatening Rockman's relationship with Michelle. The man heaved a deep sigh. Frustration simmered in his gut.

The sinking sensation in the hollow of his stomach seemed to be magnified. His hand dropped to the bouquet of flowers that rested on the passenger seat beside him. Fingering the gift card one last time, Rockman tucked the sealed mailer between the green leaves of the foliage. Exiting his vehicle he glanced quickly around to insure no one was watching as he rushed to drop his present at Michelle's front door.

Michelle's head was spinning. Everything that had made sense to her no longer fit the puzzle of her life. She'd left them all in Mark's library, retreating back up the massive stairwell to Mark's bedroom. During the short span of time the two had been meeting with Vanessa and Simon, the family's housekeeper had slipped into the room and had made up the king-size bed.

Pulling back the large comforter, Michelle slipped her fully clothed body between the freshly washed bedsheets and pulled the covers up over her head. Just hours earlier she and Mark had been in a state of bliss beside each other, no one and nothing intruding on their time together. Now, nothing Michelle had ever been comfortable with made any sense.

Michelle couldn't fathom her uncle Greg ever having done

anything to harm her father. Michelle couldn't remember a time when the two men had ever been at odds with each other and definitely not over her mother. Her mother. Michelle heaved a deep sigh.

Michelle felt nothing but indifference when she thought about Olivia Coleman. She had never harbored much emotion at all about the woman who'd given birth to her. Her father had never showed Michelle an ounce of animosity about her mother having abandoned them and so Michelle had never grown up caring about the woman one way or another. Brent Coleman had more than made up for Olivia's absence and Michelle had never wanted for anything, not even her mother's love. So why, after all the time that had passed between them, did her mother seem to hold the answers to her father's demise and the tribulations that were plaguing her? Michelle couldn't help but ponder everything she knew and everything she didn't know about the time the trio had shared together and apart from each other over the years.

Michelle could count on one hand the number of times she'd seen her mother after she left the family and even after counting she would have fingers left over. Olivia had shown up for two major events in Michelle's life; her high school graduation and her father's funeral. With each appearance Michelle would never have known she were there if it were not for Simon pointing the woman out to her.

At her graduation Olivia had stood in the back of the auditorium, standing alone until moments after Michelle had walked across the stage for her diploma. Before Michelle could imagine a conversation between them Olivia had disappeared out of sight, leaving a card and gift for her in her father's hands. Michelle had briefly imagined throwing them both into the trash but her father's reprimand had reminded her that she'd been raised better than that. Her father had had the most forgiving heart of any man she'd ever known and because he could still smile when he said her mother's name, Michelle had been able to smile with him. Her mother's gift still lay secreted away in the top drawer of her bureau.

The last time Michelle had run into her mother had been at the Greenwood Funeral Home before her father's home-going service. Olivia had been standing over the man's casket, a single red rose in her hand as tears streamed down her face. The two women had looked at each other, neither saying a word and then Olivia had swept past Michelle, racing for the exit door. Michelle still remembered her mother's lingering touch as the woman had pressed a manicured hand against Michelle's arm, extending her condolences as if she were only a family acquaintance. And then both her father and her mother were gone from her for good.

Michelle was lost in thought, preoccupied with remembrances that had turned painful, when Mark entered the room. Staring down at her, Mark could feel her angst, understanding that Michelle was feeling lost in the magnitude of her problems. He kicked off his leather shoes and crawled beneath the covers beside her. Wrapping his body around hers, Mark could almost feel the tension ebb from her body as Michelle relaxed into his arms, allowing him to bear the weight of her burdens.

Mark called her by her given name. "Michelle?"

She pressed her face into the pillow to hide the sheen of tears that teased her eyes. When she answered, her voice was husky with emotion. "Please, Mark, I would really rather not talk about it right now."

He hesitated, slowly stroking the length of her arm with his hand. "I understand, baby."

She nodded slowly. "Thank you."

They lay in silence, staring out into space. When Michelle finally closed her eyes, drifting off into a peaceful sleep she finally knew what she had to do. And she trusted that Mark would be right by her side when she needed him to be.

Chapter 22

Mark hadn't blinked an eye when Michelle had asked to visit her mother. It didn't take a rocket scientist to understand what a significant moment this was for her, so he didn't think twice about making their reunion happen as quickly as he could.

Michelle had barely washed her face and brushed her teeth before Mark had made the necessary phone calls to get their trip started. By the time Michelle had showered and changed the Stallion jet was prepped, fueled and waiting on the tarmac. The two were high in the air before their bacon-and-eggs breakfast could digest. Michelle had been staring out the plane's window ever since takeoff, conversation waning between them.

Mark could only imagine that Michelle was thinking about what she would say to the woman who was a stranger to her. He had often wondered what he might say to his own mother if such a thing were possible but since it wasn't he couldn't begin to find anything that might have been of some use to Michelle in her own quest. Reaching for Michelle's hand, he gently caressed the back of her clenched fist, stalling the shaky nerves that had Michelle quivering as though she were cold.

The flight from Dallas, Texas, to Tucson, Arizona, was ultrasmooth, the Stallion aircraft gliding toward its destination. Mark knew they would be landing within the hour and then the real drama would begin.

When the two of them had finally woken the night before, it had been dark outside. A full moon seemed to hang precariously in a blue-black sky. From the balcony outside of Mark's bedroom the view had been glorious, a spattering of stars sparkling above them. Michelle had stood outside staring skyward as she'd leaned back against Mark's bare chest, his arms wrapped protectively around her.

Conversation had flowed easily, both casual and intense, as they had shared more and more of themselves with each other. Michelle had recalled memories of her mother and her childhood. She'd cried softly as she'd recalled the day of her father's death, Mark wiping her tears away with the back of his fingers.

For the first time since forever, Mark had talked about his parents and the tragic accident that had taken them from him and his brothers. Mark had never shared his feelings about that time in his life with anyone except his brothers, but opening up to Michelle had come as easily as breathing.

Mark couldn't imagine a mother who wouldn't have wanted to be in his or his brothers' lives. Irene Stallion had been the love of all their lives, epitomizing everything that was soft and sweet and made of pure gold. She'd had the most giving spirit of any woman Mark had ever known, devoting every ounce of her time and energy wherever she was needed.

Her boys had always been front and center in her mind and her heart. Mark smiled as he remembered the wealth of kisses and hugs and touches of affection that the woman had showered down on them all.

Mark remembered his parents being the perfect complement to each other. His father, David Stallion, had been stern and commanding, with only one weakness: Mark's mother. The couple had loved a lifetime in a short time and Mark realized he wanted that for himself and he wanted it with Michelle.

Leaning toward her, Mark pressed a gentle kiss to her forehead, meeting her gaze as she turned to stare up at him. "What do you need me to do for you?" he asked softly, reaching to brush a stray hair out of her eye.

Michelle shook her head. "Just hold my hand," she answered, a slight smile pulling at her mouth. "Just hold my hand and I'll get through this."

Mark entwined his fingers with hers. "I can do that," he said, squeezing her hand beneath his.

Michelle smiled, the gesture flooding warmth over her face. Mark was in awe, marveling at how beautiful Michelle was when she smiled, the wealth of it shimmering in her eyes.

The limousine ride from the private airstrip through Tucson's main streets took less than thirty minutes before they were pulling into the driveway of Olivia Coleman's Spanish-style home. At Mark's urging, Simon had called ahead to warn her they were coming. Mark knew this was going to be difficult for both of them and he didn't want any unnecessary surprises thrown at either woman.

Olivia stood in the doorway of her home as the limo pulled up in front of the house. Her arms were crossed over her chest, her nerves on edge. She'd dreamed of this day more times than she cared to count and now that the moment was here, her daughter coming to see her, she didn't know what to say or do.

Side by side, the couple was mesmerizing. As they stepped from the limo, both staring at the landscape around them, Olivia couldn't help but notice how beautiful they were together. The tall black man looked like a male model who'd just stepped off the cover of an upscale fashion magazine. He was tall, dark and handsome, an intoxicating drink of dark chocolate in a white dress shirt worn casually over designer jeans and Timberland boots. Her only child wore a simple slip dress and canvas slip-ons. The sporty styling fit her petite frame nicely. Olivia marveled at just how exquisite a woman her little girl had grown into. A wave of sadness passed over her as she reflected on all she had missed of Michelle growing up. Olivia fought to not let the sudden wave of unhappy emotion consume her.

The man stood protectively at her daughter's side, a palm resting warmly against the young woman's lower back. There was no missing the looks of love that passed between them, his dark stare so intense that another woman could only imagine what that might feel like. Olivia remembered a man looking at her like that once, and thoughts of Michelle's father floated through her mind.

Stepping out onto the front stoop, Olivia tossed up a hesitant hand and waved, a welcoming smile filling her face. The outside air was just shy of being balmy, warmer temperatures promising to rise quickly. In the distance, the low mountain ranges beckoned for attention. The duo stared in the woman's direction, Michelle hesitating for just a quick second before strolling boldly in her mother's direction. Olivia met her halfway.

"Hi," Michelle said, her voice sounding strange to her own ear.

"Hello, Michelle," Olivia said.

A pregnant pause filled the space between them. Mark gave them both some time, allowing each to take in the moment. He extended his hand. "Mrs. Coleman, my name's Mark Stallion. I'm a friend of your daughter's."

Olivia lost her own hand beneath the man's firm grip. "It's a pleasure to meet you, Mr. Stallion."

"Please, call me Mark."

She smiled sweetly, her gaze returning to Michelle's face. "Would you like to come inside?" she asked, gesturing to the home behind her.

Michelle nodded, cutting a quick eye in Mark's direction. The man nodded his support as they followed behind their hostess.

The home was nothing like Michelle had envisioned. The warm space was a wealth of color, shades of terracotta, gold and emerald-green decorating the interior. Colorful paintings having Native American influences adorned the walls. A screened porch housed what was obviously her mother's studio, the aroma of paint wafting through the air, an unfinished canvas resting atop an easel, and cans of brushes and assorted art supplies occupying a wall of bookshelves. Michelle had known nothing about her mother's talent.

"You're very good," she said, stopping to admire the paintings that were signed with her mother's name.

"Thank you."

"I didn't know you painted."

"I didn't. Not until I came here."

Michelle nodded. The reality of her mother's life, a life that had not included her or her father suddenly slapped her, spinning her offside. She suddenly needed to sit down, dropping into a wicker chair that rested in a far corner. Both Olivia and Mark stared at her, concern washing over their expressions.

"Why did you leave us?"

Olivia took a deep breath. It was the one question she'd expected. It was also the one question she really didn't have an answer for. "Your father and I were very young when we married, Michelle. Neither of us was ready for the responsibilities."

"And so you left?"

"I had a lot of growing up to do. I couldn't do that there. I couldn't do that and support what your father wanted for his life while ignoring what I wanted for mine."

"But you left me."

"No. I left Brent. He and I made the decision that you would be better off with him caring for you than you would have been with me."

"Why didn't you contact me?"

Olivia sighed, her hands twisting nervously in front of her. "I've made a lot of mistakes, Michelle, and that was probably my biggest. If I could go back and do it all over again I would do it differently. But I can't. I regret that I hurt you. I never wanted that to happen. I love you very much. All I wanted was what was best for you."

Mark was leaning in the entranceway staring from one to the other. He couldn't begin to imagine what Michelle was feeling in that moment and he fought the desire to rush to her side to wrap her in a hug. He understood that there were some things Michelle would have to do alone and he sensed that this moment with her mother was one of those things. As if she had read his thoughts, Michelle suddenly looked in his direction, giving him a nervous smile. The look he sent her back was like a warm blanket being thrown around her shoulders.

Michelle rose from where she was seated and moved to his side. She leaned into his chest, inhaling deeply. Mark smelled of expensive cologne, the intoxicating aroma tickling her senses. She pressed her palms to his chest, peering up into his face.

"I need to talk to my mother alone. Do you think you could give us some privacy?"

"Whatever you need, sweetheart," Mark answered, smiling warmly. "I'll be in the limo."

He reached out, brushing his thumb across her lower lip. Michelle closed her eyes as Mark bent to kiss her mouth, the gesture so tender that she could feel her insides beginning to melt. Her gaze followed him as he walked out of the home. When he had disappeared from sight, Michelle turned her attention back to her mother.

As he settled himself down to wait, it didn't take long for Mark to realize that Michelle's conversation with her mother would probably go on for some time. The two women had over twenty years of talking to make up for.

With nothing else to do but wait, Mark conducted business from the backseat of the limo, catching up on the telephone calls that he'd ignored since his accident. The first was to the doctor whose follow-up appointment he'd missed and rescheduled twice, once again promising the nurse on the other end that he would make the next appointment without fail.

The second call was to his brothers to check in and let them know where he was and what he was doing. He could hear the concern in John's voice although his big brother voiced nothing but support. Matthew and Luke both sent words of advice and encouragement his way. As Mark disconnected the call he grinned, just imagining the conversation the trio was having about him and Michelle. It hadn't been that long since he, Matthew and Luke had been talking about John and Marah.

Mark shook his head. It was hard to believe that just a few short months ago he would never have imagined himself settled down with any one woman and now he couldn't imagine himself not being settled down with Michelle.

He knew that there was nothing in the world that he wouldn't do for Michelle Coleman. The intensity of emotion he was feeling for her was like nothing he'd known before. He loved Michelle. Time had done that to him and now all he wanted was to do whatever was necessary to make things good for her.

Mark's next call was to Vanessa. The woman's excitement assaulted him over the telephone line.

"It's about time you called me back," Vanessa chastised. "What took you so long?"

"Vanessa, you are always so impatient."

"People sure love to gossip when you give them something juicy to gossip about!" the woman exclaimed excitedly.

"What's going on?"

"I have three eyewitnesses who can place your boy Rockman in the garage alone with your bike just before your accident. And I have two other eyewitnesses who swear he was around the garage when that Dooley fellow had his accident. In fact, Dooley remembers Rockman being in his space alone just before his race.

"My eyewitnesses all talked to that phony detective and told them what they saw and he ignored them. So I called in a favor from my friend at the district attorney's office."

"You have a friend at the D.A.'s office?"

Vanessa giggled. "She's a new friend actually."

Mark shook his head. "Okay, I-Spy."

"I really missed my calling. I make one heck of a private investigator, boy, if I do say so myself."

Mark laughed. "So what did this new friend have to say?"

"It's not what honey said. It's what she was able to do. Your two boys in blue have been suspended pending an investigation. It appears that there is one heck of an electronic paper trail connecting them to Rockman."

"What about the charges against Michelle?"

"She's working on them. There's a new team investigating the case now."

"I do like the way you work, Vanessa!"

Mark could feel his friend smiling widely on the other end.

"How's your girl?" Vanessa inquired, concern reflected in her tone.

He felt himself shrug, his broad shoulders pushing toward the vehicle's roof. "Holding her own," Mark answered.

Vanessa nodded into the receiver. "She'll be fine," the woman said softly. "You've got her back so she'll be just fine."

Mark smiled. "See you soon, Vanessa."

"Later!"

An hour later the front door to Olivia's home swung slowly open. Mark stepped out of the limo, staring toward the entrance at Michelle and her mother, the two women still locked in conversation. He could tell that they both had been crying profusely, eyes puffed red, stealing glances in his direction. As he met Michelle's gaze his heartbeat kicked up several notches.

Michelle looked battle weary but there was a glow of contentment across her face that hadn't been there earlier. Mark's lips spread in a slow, easy grin as Michelle moved in his direction. Olivia stood at her front door smiling warmly at them both.

"Hey you," Mark said softly as Michelle met him with a huge hug. The scene was surreal, like something out of a movie as the two greeted each other like they'd been separated for years.

Michelle smiled into his eyes. "Hey yourself. Are you okay?"

Mark chuckled. "I should be asking you that."

"I'm with you now. I'm just fine," she said, nuzzling his throat with her nose as she basked in the familiar scent of him.

Olivia tossed them a quick wave of her hand before doing an about-face. She moved back inside her home, turning to look at them. Mark nodded his goodbye, his gaze shuffling from mother to daughter as Michelle smiled back at her before the door closed.

Their eyes met again, Mark's inquisitive look asking if Michelle wanted to share the experience with him.

"I don't hate her," Michelle said, looking back toward her mother's home. "Maybe one day I'll come see her again."

An hour later Mark and Michelle were back in the Stallion jet headed for home.

Chapter 23

Michelle was emotionally exhausted. Leaning into Mark's shoulder, she looped her arm through his and held him close. The man kissed her forehead, brushing his face into her hair before leaning back against her, the two of them holding each other up.

Over the years Michelle had dreamed of the conversation she would one day have with the woman who had given birth to her. The talk the two had shared that morning though had gone nothing like the conversations in her mind. Her mother had been nothing like Michelle had imagined her to be.

Olivia Coleman made no apologies for her actions. The woman had made peace with the decisions in her life and though she acknowledged the few regrets she held, both knew, without it being said, that she would do it all over again if she needed to.

Because of her father, Michelle had never faulted her mother for leaving. It seemed that Brent had understood better than anyone why Olivia had needed to go. The two had stayed in contact with one another through the years and Michelle discovered that her father had been supportive of the choices her mother had made for her life.

It had been telling for Michelle to go through the many cards and letters the man had sent his estranged wife over the years. Michelle had been grateful for the opportunity to peek into a side of her father's life that she'd had no knowledge of. The two women had talked, laughed, argued and cried and then they'd done it again, crying until both had been all cried out. When all was said and done, Michelle understood that her mother's love for her had been unselfish, the woman making the ultimate sacrifice to do what she had believed to be best for her child. The two had politely agreed to disagree on some issues and then they'd moved on, Olivia sharing the story of Brent, Greg and herself. Michelle had found it difficult to believe that she had never been privy to the triangle that had been a thorn in her parents' side.

Her mother had cared about both men. Her mother had loved Brent like she had never loved Greg Rockman. Both of her parents had worked to maintain the childhood bonds of friendship with Rockman and despite their best efforts that friendship had soured between them.

Michelle suddenly sat upright. "Mark, look at this," she said, pulling a small envelope from her purse. "My mother gave this to me."

Mark pulled the mailer from Michelle's hands, pulling at the enclosed gift card. The small card was hand printed. Familiar wording glared up at them.

"My mother had a secret admirer, too."

Mark was suddenly shaking with jealous rage. He found himself hoping the police got to Greg Rockman before he did.

"I am really going to hurt that son of a—"

Michelle pressed her fingers to his lips, stalling the harsh words spilling out of his mouth. She leaned up to kiss his anger away. "Do we have enough to take to the police?" she asked. "Do you think they'll believe us?"

Inhaling swiftly, Mark nodded his head, relaying his earlier conversation with Vanessa. "I'm sure they will. Hopefully we'll get this mess cleared up before the week is over."

Leaning back in her seat, Michelle smiled. "Hopefully."

John Stallion stormed out of his executive office suite into the outer reception area. Juanita was seated behind the secretarial desk poring through a stack of legal documents that needed John's attention. She was taken aback by his brusqueness.

"What's the matter, John? What's happened?" the older woman asked anxiously.

John shook his head as he reached for a notepad on top of the desk. He scrawled across the bright white paper with a blue ink pen, tossing both down on the desktop in front of her as he barked out orders.

"Call Police Chief Bradley. Tell him to meet me at this address."

Juanita picked up the notepad and nodded her head. "What's going on, John?"

The man ignored the question, responding instead to the cell phone on his waist band that was beeping for his attention. Juanita watched as he read the text message that had just been sent to him, quickly responding with a text of his own. John heaved a deep sigh.

"I swear," he muttered under his breath, heading for the door.

"John Stallion, don't you dare walk out of this room until you tell me what's going on!" Juanita shouted after him, her maternal concern spilling out of her spirit.

John backtracked to her side, leaning to kiss her cheek. "Everything is going to be fine, Aunt Juanita. I'm going to make sure of that. Mark is headed over to Rockman's office and I want the police there when he arrives. I'm on my way there now."

Juanita nodded. "Should I call the other boys?" she asked.

John chuckled. "Matthew and Luke are downstairs already. I've got to go. I'll call you as soon as I know what's going on," he said as he opened the door to the exterior corridor.

"You're going to make sure everything's okay, right?"

John met the matriarch's gaze, holding it briefly. He smiled, the bend of his lips meant to be convincing. "You know I will, Aunt Juanita. Don't you worry about a thing," he said.

As he rushed to the elevator, a look of worry washed over his face. He had never promised Juanita anything before that he couldn't accomplish, but this time he wasn't so sure. There had been something in Mark's tone when he last spoke to him that hadn't sat well with John. Between his earlier conversation with Vanessa and everything Mark had just told him he didn't see any confrontation between Mark and Greg Rockman playing out nicely. Most especially since Mark didn't have a clue about all else that had happened over the past twenty-four hours.

Michelle didn't like the way this was starting to feel. Mark had barely spoken two words during the ride from the airport to her town house. The two sat inside his car as he tapped anxiously at the steering wheel.

"You were trying to break a few speeding records there, weren't you?" Michelle asked facetiously.

Mark shrugged his shoulders. "Sorry about that."

"Let's go inside," Michelle said, resting her hand atop his

forearm. "There's probably nothing in the refrigerator but we can order a pizza if you're hungry."

The man leaned to kiss her cheek. "Go on inside," he said. "I'll be right back. I have an errand to run."

Michelle sat staring at him, the two eyeing each other with reservation. She shook her head, her hair waving from side to side. "Maybe we should go down to the station tonight and talk to those detectives instead." She glanced down at her wristwatch. "It's still early."

Mark nodded. "This won't take long, Mitch. I promise. And the detectives are expecting you first thing in the morning."

"Mark, promise me that you're not going to go see Rockman. Please. Just let the police handle this!" Michelle implored.

Mark leaned to kiss her a second time, brushing his mouth against her mouth. He shook his head. "I love you, Michelle. You know that, don't you?"

She nodded, pressing her palm to the side of his face. "I love you, too. I love you very much."

Mark grinned widely. "I hear there's a NASCAR race on tonight. Warm up my side of the sofa and I'll be right back to watch it with you. Okay?"

Michelle shook her head. "You aren't going to promise me, are you?"

Warm breath blew past the man's lips as the two locked gazes. Mark could see that Michelle wasn't but so happy with him right then. He closed his eyes, then opened them quickly to stare at her again. He smiled.

"I promise you that I won't do anything stupid. Okay?"

Michelle nodded. "Did you call your brother?"

Mark's head bobbed up and down. "Yes, and I assure you that John won't let me get into any trouble," he said. "So, are we good with each other?"

Michelle nodded, but wasn't convinced she trusted that Mark would keep his promise to her.

"Bring back some burgers," she said as she exited the car, leaning to peer into the window. "And don't forget the French fries!"

Michelle watched as Mark sped out of the parking lot. She stood staring behind him until he was well out of sight. Turning, she headed toward her front door. She couldn't believe that it had been five days since she'd last seen the inside of her home. It amazed her how life could spin so out of control when you least expected it.

Pushing her key into the front door lock, she couldn't help but think about Mark and Rockman and everything she'd learned about her mother and father over the past twenty-four hours. She couldn't wait to call her uncle Simon to see if he could fill in the remaining blanks that still had her confused about some of the details.

As she closed and locked the door behind her, Michelle was completely lost in thought. As she switched on the interior lights it took her a moment to notice the cascade of flowers that covered every visible surface from her kitchen to her living room. The succulent aroma of roses filled the air, teasing her senses as she stood staring in disbelief. And something else teased her nostrils as well, a hint of gasoline seeming to waft around the room. Michelle wrinkled her nose.

Dropping her keys onto the foyer table, Michelle sauntered from one room to the other in shock. The scene was like nothing she'd ever seen before, her entire home a formidable garden of every kind of flower imaginable. Roses, lilies, irises and tulips littered the counters. Daffodils, orchids and daisies rested in containers on the floor. Carnations, snapdragons and asters rested on top of the tables. It was suddenly haunting and a wave of fear gripped Michelle's heart.

She moved to find the telephone, knowing the receiver had been sitting in its terminal on the top of her desk. It was only when she'd moved to the center of her living room that she saw Greg Rockman sitting in the corner watching her. And that was when Michelle screamed.

Chapter 24

When Mark pulled into the corporate parking lot for Rockman Racing, his brothers were standing in conversation with the local police. Blue lights flashed atop resting patrol cars as a crew of uniformed officers waited patiently for instructions.

John rushed forward to meet him as he made his way to their side.

"What's up?" Mark said.

"We're running a little interference. Are you okay?" his older sibling asked.

Mark nodded. "Where is he?"

Matthew and Luke joined them. "No one knows," Matthew answered. "The cops have been looking for him since yesterday. There was a fire down at the Stallion garages. Two of the mechanics saw him leaving the scene and they found his fingerprints on a gas can dropped at the site."

"A fire? No one was hurt, were they?" Mark asked, looking from one brother another.

Luke shook his head. "No, but you're down another three bikes. Those things melt quick!"

Mark cursed out loud, profanity filtering through the air. "So, where do they think he is?" he asked, turning to the chief of police, who was listening to their conversation.

John's friend shook his head. "We've issued a warrant for his arrest. My men will find him," the officer professed.

Mark turned, his hands gripping the sides of his waist. Maybe it was better that he hadn't found Rockman, he thought to himself. He turned back around as another officer came rushing up to his superior. The two men stood in hushed discussion before the second officer rushed back into the building he'd just left.

The Stallion men all stared, asking the same question in unison. "What's going on?"

Chief Bradley shook his head. "Do any of you know where we can find Michelle Coleman?" he questioned, looking directly at Mark.

"Why? What's going on?" Mark asked.

The officer held up a hand that was meant to be calming. His tone was even and controlled, the urgency of the situation suppressed to the best of his ability. "We want to put an officer on her, just in case. We have reason to believe…"

Before the man could finish his statement, Mark sprinted back to his car and jumped inside. As his brothers rushed to follow him, he gunned the engine and burned rubber out of the parking lot, racing to get back across town to Michelle.

Michelle sat bound and gagged while Rockman walked a slow circle around her. She couldn't believe this was happening to her. Her look was pleading as she stared at him, begging for him to just talk to her. Michelle was desperate to make sense of what was going on.

Rockman hadn't uttered a word since he'd jumped from his seat, slapping Michelle into silence. He was hoping against all odds that none of her neighbors had heard her scream and no one would be knocking on her front door to see if she was all right.

He needed more time. Everything had happened too fast and he'd been careless. Being reckless had proved to be his downfall, one mistake leading to another and another. Now they were looking for him, wanting to ask him questions about fires and accidents and people being injured and killed. This wasn't how it was supposed to have ended. It wasn't supposed to have been him caught in the crossfire.

The man shook, the gun in his hand waving from side to side. Michelle stared at the weapon and then Rockman's face, wishing he would just let her talk so that she could try to calm him down. It was obvious that the Uncle Greg she'd known and loved wasn't himself. The man who stood terrorizing her wasn't a man she knew.

Rockman rushed to the window, peering out the closed blinds to the parking lot below. There was no movement, nothing out of the ordinary to draw his attention. He let the blinds fall back into place and resumed his pacing, walking a circular path across her hardwood floors.

Michelle didn't have a clue how much time had passed, minutes feeling like hours. She could hear her cell phone ringing in her purse although Rockman seemed oblivious to the noise. When the man finally spoke, she was startled, the harsh tone of his voice like nothing she'd ever heard before.

"This is all your fault," he boomed. "It didn't have to be

like this." He pointed the gun in Michelle's direction, then allowed it to fall back to his side. "I love you," the man ranted. "All you had to do was love me back."

Michelle's eyes filled with tears that threatened to spill over her cheeks. She nodded her head, her gaze moving Rockman to resume his pacing.

"Okay. Okay. Okay," Rockman chanted. "I can fix this. This can still work," he said, his eyes flitting back and forth in their sockets. "This isn't so bad. No one knows anything. All the evidence is circumstantial," the man reasoned.

Michelle nodded and he paused to stare down at her.

"Why did you have to keep digging? Just like your mother. Never satisfied to just let things go."

Confusion painted Michelle's expression as the man continued to rant at her.

"The first time it was an accident. I didn't mean for Brent's bike to explode. Olivia wouldn't leave it alone. Always asking questions. Always in the way. Looking at me like I'd done it on purpose. It wasn't like he was hurt or anything. It didn't even faze him. He was right back on a bike the following week.

"And then she started hammering at him. Telling him I couldn't be trusted. Brent trusted me. He was my best friend and then she came along and it all changed. I tried to make her my girl and she wouldn't have it. She loved him instead. She couldn't love me. She didn't trust me and after everything I did for her. No one else ever sent her flowers."

He paused, taking a deep breath as he seemed to drift off into memories of a past Michelle knew very little about. When he came back to the moment he was ranting again.

"It didn't even faze him!"

Neither of them heard the commotion in the lot below. Rockman was lost as he reflected back on his time with

Michelle's father and mother, a time that had led him to where he now stood. Michelle could only see the gun he continued to wave obliviously in front of her as he talked nonsensically about everything and about nothing.

"I fixed them both. I did. You loved me, Mitch. They couldn't keep you from loving me. Brent tried. He did but I stopped him. I stopped him good that time.

"Bam!" the man exclaimed, slapping his hands together as he shouted at the top of his lungs. He began to laugh and cry simultaneously, all rationality lost to him. He seemed to be rocking back and forth where he stood, tears streaming down his face into his beard. "I did that. Made sure he couldn't stop you from loving me. He stopped your mother. He did that good. But I fixed him."

The man's expression suddenly changed. Hostility washed over his spirit, his earlier anger resurfacing with a vengeance. "Then you had to start asking questions. Why couldn't you just let things go? Huh, Mitch? Why? I sent you flowers! See!" Rockman shouted, his arms flailing out to his sides as he pointed at the floral arrangements that filled the space. "Didn't you like the flowers and the dinner? I did that for you, Mitch. Me. Not Stallion. What did he ever do for you? He didn't love you like I loved you."

The man slammed his weapon down harshly against the television top. The glass screen shattered. Michelle's eyes widened with fear as Rockman stared at the mess he had made, seeming to be startled by what had happened. In that moment neither heard the front door opening and closing. Neither of them was paying any attention to the team of law enforcement officers that had let themselves into her home. Not until they called Rockman's name and ordered him to put down his weapon.

Chapter 25

Mark was gunning the engine of his Gold Wing, pushing the limits of time and speed as he made his way down the highway. Beside him, Michelle was holding her own, the Harley Sportster she was driving moving with ease beside him.

The duo had been on the road for two days, the cross-country trip coming after Michelle had been cleared of all charges. The teams at the track were still gossiping about the hoopla surrounding Greg Rockman and his involvement in the death of Brent Coleman and the kidnapping of Brent's daughter, Mitch.

Michelle heaved a deep sigh as they crossed the border into South Carolina, headed for the sand in Myrtle Beach. She and Mark had jumped at his brother's suggestion that they get away for some serious rest and relaxation. John had given Mark a nod of approval and the two had disappeared before anyone had realized they were gone. Since pulling out of the driveway of the Stallion family home, the trip had been surreal.

Michelle wiggled her fingers, relishing the feel of the new diamond ring on her ring finger. The expensive trinket felt awkward beneath her riding gloves but she couldn't ever imagine taking it off her hand. Mark had placed it there just hours earlier as they'd ridden through Louisiana, stopping by the home of a family friend who just happened to be a judge in the county of Orleans. With a picture ID and certified copies of their birth certificates, the duo was issued a marriage license in minutes, that family friend pronouncing them husband and wife in a quick civil ceremony.

Michelle was still in awe of the moment. The two had stood hand in hand, dressed in biker leathers, laughing as if they didn't have a care in the world. Mark had balked at her suggestion that they call his family and hers first to let them know their intentions. It hadn't taken much to convince Michelle that eloping was the best thing in the world for them to do.

Now she was Mrs. Mark Stallion, married to the most incredible man she could have imagined. As Mark had kissed her after the impromptu ceremony, Michelle couldn't wish for anything more, the promise of their future together gleaming brightly from both their eyes.

She laughed out loud, sheer joy filling her as Mark pointed in the direction of a Marriott Hotel right off the interstate. Shutting down her engine, she shifted the bike back on its kickstand, securing it for the night. Mark stood with his hand extended toward her as she swung her leg up and over the vehicle, standing by its side.

"How was that ride!" Mark exclaimed, removing his helmet from his head.

Michelle grinned. "You were a little slow on the uptake there. What happened?"

Mark laughed. "I got slow for you, woman! Let me show you slow!"

He pulled her into his arms and kissed her, his tongue eagerly searching for the back of her throat. They held the kiss for some time and when they finally broke the connection, coming back up for air, both were breathing heavily.

"That was very nice!" Michelle exclaimed, pressing her free palm to his chest.

Mark grinned. "It's my wedding night. Girl, I've got all kinds of tricks up my sleeve!"

The two laughed warmly, nuzzling against each other. "Now who's the one trying to start something?" Michelle said, her voice low and seductive. She giggled as Mark nibbled against her neck, his tongue lapping hungrily at the flesh beneath her chin. "Now you know you need to stop!"

Mark purred. It was a deep hum that rose from his midsection into her ear. "Woman, you better check me in to a hotel room and check me in quick. I've got something for you!"

Minutes later, Mr. and Mrs. Mark Stallion were headed up the elevator to the only available room in the entire hotel. Two senior citizens occupied the space with them, both going on about their last bingo game as Mark and Michelle stood listening. Mark's stare was undeniable, shooting daggers of lust in her direction behind the two gray-headed people and Michelle couldn't help but grin widely.

The elevator stopped on the ninth floor and the seniors made their exit, turning to wish them both a nice evening.

Mark laughing, grinning as he waved. "It's my wedding night!" he chimed, his voice carrying as the door closed between them.

Michelle's laughter filled the small space. Before she could comment Mark spun her around toward him, cupping his hands around the back of her neck. He kissed her softly and Michelle couldn't keep herself from kissing him back. She clutched the front of the leather jacket he was wearing, pulling him to her as she slipped her arms around his waist, working her mouth over his mouth.

Mark had an incredible mouth. He licked her upper lip and then her bottom, suckling the flesh hungrily. Dropping his helmet to the floor, Mark slipped his hands into her hair, his fingertips meeting behind her head as he held her to him, his mouth still working magic over hers. When the elevator door opened on the twelfth floor Michelle pulled herself out of his arms.

"Where are you going?" Mark asked, his arms extended toward her. "I liked that!"

Michelle laughed. "So did I but if you want more you're gonna have to catch me!" she said as she ran in the direction of their room.

With a wide smile filling his face, Mark groaned, racing down the length of corridor behind her. By the time Michelle had reached the room's door, sliding the electronic door key through the register, Mark had caught up with her. Michelle squealed with glee as Mark wrapped her in a deep bear hug. Pushing their way into the room, Mark turned to lock the door behind them as Michelle fell across the bed.

Falling down beside her, Mark pulled her arms over her head, holding her by the wrists as he kissed her again. Every nerve ending in Michelle's body was on fire, heat radiating from the center of her core. She wiggled excitedly beneath the man.

"How about a shower," she whispered as Mark left a damp trail of kisses across her cheeks, past the line of her ear, down to her neck.

He nodded, still humming his appreciation against her

skin. "I can do that," he said, his hands pulling at her clothes. "Let me help you out of these clothes."

"Fine," Michelle giggled as he unbuttoned her leather pants and slipped them down to her knees. Mark dropped to the floor, still pulling at her clothes as Michelle pulled one leg and then another out of the pant legs. Michelle moved to push her panties over her hips and as she did Mark slapped her hands away.

"I don't need any help!" he said, shaking his index finger at her. Michelle laughed again as he pulled the garment down past her sex and over her legs. Michelle's eyes opened wide as Mark's hands instinctively moved to the outside of her thighs, gently caressing the soft flesh. Lifting herself upward, she smiled down at him.

"If you keep doing that we're not going to make it to the shower," Michelle said, her eyebrows raised.

Mark shrugged his shoulders, saying nothing as he began to kiss her abdomen, his tongue dipping in and out of her belly button. His touch was intoxicating and Michelle felt herself swooning as though she were faint. Before she knew it her jacket and top had been tossed to the floor, Michelle lying completely naked against the hotel bedspread.

Mark had moved back above her, covering her body with his own. The two were moving slowly against each other and Michelle couldn't think of anything but Mark's touch. She moaned his name over and over again as if in prayer, heat rising rapidly between them.

Skilled fingers danced against her flesh, Mark drawing slow easy circles from the bottom of her rib cage to the top of her pubic bone. His touch was soothing, relaxing every ounce of tension from her body. Michelle's nipples reacted, the sensitive buds hardening without being touched. Michelle could feel them tingling for attention and she pulled a casual hand across her breast. Mark laughed, his face pressed into her abdomen.

"You're a tease," Michelle hissed, her smile widening.

Mark shook his head. "Nope. Just getting you ready for your shower."

Michelle moaned, unable to answer as Mark's fingertips collided with one stiff nipple. He held it there for a brief minute then resumed the gentle massage. A soft moan eased past Michelle's lips. The stimulation caused a contraction deep in the center of Michelle's feminine spirit and she inhaled swiftly.

Mark continued to touch her, fingers dancing against her flesh, his mouth and tongue following his touch. It was suddenly warmer than Michelle had remembered it being. Perspiration beaded across her brow, between her breasts and thighs and Michelle could feel herself opening her legs widely wishing for a cool breeze to bring her some relief. A deep shudder went through her whole body.

She reached for him, pulling at the clothes he was still dressed in. Michelle was suddenly hungry for more of him, desperate to feel his naked flesh against her own. For the second time Mark pushed her hands away, waving his finger from side to side.

"Patience, Mrs. Stallion," he said as Michelle struggled to speak.

Words failed her, her attention focused on his ministrations. The man had her breathing heavily with wanting and Michelle couldn't begin to imagine the moment ever ending.

He put his hands under her knees and lifted her feet until they were flat on the mattress. Moving his palms to the top of her knees, Mark gently applied pressure. "Open up for me," he commanded, his husky voice like a smooth liqueur.

Michelle could feel her thighs yielding to his touch. Her sex opened like a rose in full bloom. The sweet nectar that had been dammed up now flowed with complete abandon. Michelle could feel Mark's fingers dancing in the slick moisture and she stifled a scream as he touched her.

Mark's hands continued moving against her, his fingers gliding in and out of her secret garden as though he were searching for something. When he arrived at his target, the resulting sensation started a low rumbling that seemed to swell from someplace deep in her midsection.

"Oh, Mark," Michelle said through clenched teeth, clutching the bedspread in the palms of her hands. Michelle knew she was at a point of no return, feeling a distinct pounding in her crotch. She tried to hold back the building orgasm but Mark's thumb was tapping like magic against her throbbing pleasure button. Michelle exploded, her hips bucking several times as she screamed his name. Her body was racked with one spasm after another, the waves of pleasure seeming to go on and on.

When Michelle finally stopped shaking, the last muscle twitching out of control, Mark rose from where he was sitting. Michelle lifted her torso onto her elbows as she watched him step out of his clothes. The man was still grinning at her. As he moved toward the bathroom doorway, Michelle called after him.

"And what was that, Mr. Stallion?"

The man tossed her a quick wink. "That Mrs. Stallion was me getting you ready for that shower you wanted," he said, turning his naked backside to her.

Michelle couldn't help but smile at the view, the taut muscles of his back and buttocks beckoning to her.

Inside the bathroom, Mark stood waiting for the flow of water to turn warm. Michelle moved to his side, wrapping her arms tightly around his waist as Mark hugged her to him. He leaned to kiss her lips, allowing his mouth to linger lightly against hers.

"I love you," Michelle said, meeting his gaze evenly.

Mark nodded his head, dropping his cheek to hers. "I love you, too," he whispered into her ear, pulling her into the warm spray of water beside him.

Hours later Mark was sleeping peacefully beside her. Michelle knew that when he woke they would make love again and again until they were ready to climb back onto their bikes and continue on their journey. Michelle had never imagined a fantasy romance like the one she shared with the man beside her, but Mark was truly a dream come true. As he snored softly, Michelle trailed a light finger along his profile, trailing a path across his lips. The moment couldn't have been more perfect, the young woman thought, blanketing his body with her own.

Michelle felt a wide smile pulling at her mouth as she stared at the ring on her finger. Who would have ever figured she would be Mrs. Michelle Stallion, wife and mechanic. Grinning, she closed her eyes, slowly drifting off to sleep. Taming a wild stallion hadn't been at all what she had imagined it would be, she thought, every ounce of Mark's love sweeping over her spirit.

Wrong DRESS, Right GUY

Award-winning author
SHIRLEY HAILSTOCK

Cinnamon Scott can't resist trying on the gorgeous wedding dress mistakenly sent to her. When MacKenzie Grier arrives to retrieve his sister's missing gown, he's floored by this angelic vision...and his own longings. With sparks like these flying, can the altar be far off?

"Shirley Hailstock again displays her tremendous storytelling ability with *My Lover, My Friend.*"
—*Romantic Times BOOKreviews*

Coming the first week of June wherever books are sold.

KIMANI™
ROMANCE

Destined *to* MEET

Acclaimed author
devon vaughn archer

When homebody Courtney Hudson busts loose for one
night, she winds up in bed with sexy Lloyd Vance, an
Alaskan cop escaping a troubled past. Then tragedy strikes
and they're caught in a twist of fate that threatens
to destroy their burgeoning love.

"[*Christmas Heat*] has wonderful,
well-written characters and a story that flows."
—*Romantic Times BOOKreviews*

Coming the first week of June wherever books are sold.

KIMANI™
ROMANCE

These women are about to discover that every passion
has a price...and some secrets are impossible to keep.

NATIONAL BESTSELLING AUTHOR

ROCHELLE ALERS

After Hours

A deliciously scandalous novel that brings together
three very different women, united by the secret lives
they lead. Adina, Sybil and Karla all lead seemingly
charmed, luxurious lives, yet each also harbors a
surprising secret that is about to spin out of control.

"Alers paints such vivid descriptions that when Jolene
becomes the target of a murderer, you almost feel
as though someone you know is in great danger."
—*Library Journal* on *No Compromise*

*Coming the first week of March
wherever books are sold.*

sepia™

NATIONAL BESTSELLING AUTHOR

ROCHELLE ALERS

invites you to meet the Whitfields of New York....

Tessa, Faith and Simone Whitfield know all about coordinating
other people's weddings, and not so much about arranging
their own love lives. But in the space of one unforgettable year,
all three will meet intriguing men who just might bring them their
very own happily ever after....

Long Time Coming
June 2008

The Sweetest Temptation
July 2008

Taken by Storm
August 2008

ARABESQUE®